Changing the Past

by

Shawna Delacorte

Changing the Past

Cover Art by *Diana Carlile*

The Wild Rose Press, Inc.
PO Box 708
Adams Basin, NY 14410-0708
Visit us at www.thewildrosepress.com

Publishing History
First Edition, 2024
Trade Paperback ISBN 978-1-5092-5479-8
Digital ISBN 978-1-5092-5480-4

Previously Published Triskelion Publishing 2007
Published in the United States of America

Praise for Author

Shawna Delacorte

"Shawna Delacorte *Who's Been Sleeping In My Bed?* has an intriguing plot and forthright characters."

~*Romantic Times*

~*~

"*The Sedgwick Curse* by Shawna Delacorte is a spine tingler from the very beginning. I spent a nail biting evening racing through the pages to a wonderfully, satisfying, aha ending. Lovers of romantic intrigue and suspense will be totally captivated by *The Sedgwick Curse*."

~*CataRomance*

~*~

"*Stormbound with a Tycoon*, Shawna Delacorte's latest, sizzles with two hot characters and an interesting storyline."

~*Romantic Times*

~*~

"*The Rocky Road to Romance* by Shawna Delacorte. This book is a sweet, feel good read. The characters are likable and the writing is good."

~*Laila K/NetGalley*

Prologue

Los Angeles, California

A feeling of blissful contentment settled over Meg Wainwright as she idly ran her fingertips over Blaine Reeves' tanned body—across his well-toned chest and down his stomach. His slightly tensed six-foot two-inch frame lay motionless, stretched out next to her. His thick, sandy-colored hair framed his handsomely chiseled features marred only by the small scar on his chin. She caught the fleeting look of foreboding that flashed across his face.

"What's wrong?" She turned on her side, a tingle of excitement darting across her bare skin as she brushed against his arm. Placing her hand on his chest, she leaned over to kiss him.

He quickly averted his gaze, then turned his face away.

"What's the matter?" She looked at him questioningly, concern touching her words combined with a sudden tremor of anxiety, almost like a sense of foreboding. "You've been very distant all evening. Are you feeling okay?"

Blaine took a deep breath, held it for a few seconds, then slowly exhaled. He spoke haltingly, the control and command he usually projected missing from his voice. "I've, uh, had a good job offer—" He nervously cleared his throat. "—from an East Coast publishing company. It's a chance to move from my current position of art director to managing editor of a magazine. I've been thinking it over," he paused a moment before continuing, his voice dropping to a near whisper, "and I've decided to accept it."

A shiver of apprehension replaced Meg's previous concern. "I don't understand." She couldn't hide her confusion. "When did all of this come about?"

"Oh…we've been talking about it for a while." He hesitated before awkwardly adding, "It starts Monday."

Meg opened her eyes wide in disbelief. Her words caught in her throat, but she managed to force them out. "*This* Monday?"

Blaine closed his eyes without responding to her question.

She quickly slid out of bed, her long legs bringing her to her five-foot seven-inch height. Her increasing sense of panic seeped into her voice and surrounded her words. "Why didn't you tell me?"

Her fingers trembled slightly as she toyed with the gold chain around her neck, a present from Blaine on the six-month anniversary of their first date.

"What about us?" Her voice quavered as the cold chill of reality settled over her, accompanied by a wave of emotional turmoil. Tears filled her eyes and threatened to trickle down her cheeks.

Blaine climbed out of bed and gently placed his hands on her shoulders. "I didn't want to upset you." He started to draw her to him and enfold her in his embrace. "We'll definitely stay in touch. I don't want to lose contact with you."

She blinked back the tears. A fiery anger shoved her

hurt and confusion aside. She backed away from his arms, her voice cloaked in disbelief. "You don't want to lose contact with me?" She couldn't keep the sarcasm hidden as she repeated her words in a louder voice. "You don't want to lose contact? Well, you'd better make sure I'm on your Christmas card list."

She turned her back on him as the tears welled in her eyes again and the stinging hurt returned.

"Meg."

She shook off his touch as he tried to turn her toward him.

"You'd better go." She fought to keep her voice controlled. "I'm sure you must have a lot of packing to do. Certainly more important things to do than being here." The full impact of the pain churned inside her. She couldn't force herself to remain close to him any longer. She fled across the bedroom into the bathroom, slamming the door behind her.

"Meg, wait." Blaine followed but found the bathroom door locked. He rapped his knuckles sharply against the door. "Meg, open up."

The only sounds coming from behind the door were sobs, quickly drowned out by the splashing of water when she turned on the shower. A quick surge of panic hit him. He continued to pound his fist against the door. His voice grew louder and more insistent. "Answer me."

The only response was the sound of running water.

He slowly leaned his forehead against the door, his eyes tightly closed and his trembling hand gripping the doorknob. In a barely audible voice, one filled with the despair rapidly engulfing him, he tried once more. "Meg…please…"

No reply came from behind the door.

His hand dropped lifelessly to his side. He reluctantly dressed, mechanically moving through the functions without being fully cognizant of what he was doing. After one last anxiety-ridden glance toward the closed bathroom door, he quietly left her apartment. He walked down the hall toward the building's outside door, his heart heavy with emotional pain—a pain for which he had to take full responsibility.

Chapter One

London, England—Ten Years Later

Sir Geoffrey Lewiston sat behind his large desk in his paneled office, very displeased with the most recent news. His dark, beady eyes glared out from his sallow, angular face. He stroked his pointed chin with his long fingers.

Sir Geoffrey was accustomed to having things his way. He didn't like it when other people interfered with his plans. And that particularly applied to the upstart American who had shown up out of nowhere and acted as if he had some sort of right to invade Sir Geoffrey's privileged territory.

He clenched his thin lips into a tightly drawn line. "I want that Sinclair deal. Who do these Pendragon people think they are? You keep that access to them open, make contact on a daily basis. I want to know every move they make."

"Won't daily contact be suspicious, especially considering she thinks I'm a traveling salesman?"

Sir Geoffrey rose from his chair and leaned across his desk, glaring at the man seated across from him. "I don't need any of your backtalk. You'll do as you're told."

****

"Miss Wainwright?" The man in his early fifties

wearing a chauffeur's uniform approached Meg as she maneuvered her baggage-laden cart out of customs at Heathrow Airport.

"Yes, I'm Meg Wainwright."

"I'm William. Dennis Mallory sent me to collect you. Is this trolley all of your luggage?"

She laughed as she looked at all the suitcases. "I sure hope so."

William transferred her luggage to the waiting limo. A few minutes later, they merged into the main flow of traffic headed eastward. The limo glided effortlessly through the rolling green countryside that quickly gave way to the crowded streets of London.

Forty-five minutes later, they came to a stop in front of the luxury hotel. The assistant manager greeted her, immediately escorting her to the suite where she had been pre-registered. A few minutes later her luggage arrived at the door.

Meg surveyed her surroundings, a bright, spacious two-room suite. The parlor contained a comfortable seating arrangement with an entertainment center including television. On the other side of the parlor, she noted a dining table with six chairs. Close to that, a standalone bar with American-style ice maker, mini refrigerator, and microwave. A desk had been positioned next to a large window offering a spectacular view of Hyde Park. There were two doors, one to a full bathroom and the other to a large bedroom with king-size bed and private bathroom.

As she unpacked the last of her clothes, room service arrived with a large floral arrangement. The accompanying card read, *Welcome to London. I'll call on you at half past seven this evening to discuss the details of the book assignment before our meeting tomorrow morning with the publisher.* The note had been signed by Dennis Mallory, Managing Editor of Pendragon Publishing.

Only nine years old, Pendragon had already become a major challenger to the long-established firms in the European marketplace, a truly remarkable success story. She had been very surprised when her agent brought her the offer to photograph and write their new line of travel books, the initial volume covering England. The exceedingly generous contract and large advance made it foolish for her to even consider turning it down.

She looked at her watch—two-thirty in the afternoon London time. Her non-stop flight from Los Angeles had her up all night. A quick nap to ward off her exhaustion would be just enough so she would be fresh and alert for her meeting with Dennis Mallory that evening. She stretched out on the bed and closed her eyes.

****

When she opened her eyes again, a surprising three hours had passed. A quick moment of panic hit her. She had intended to nap for only an hour. She hurried to get ready for her meeting. At precisely seven-thirty she opened the door to a man in his early to mid forties.

"Hello. I'm Dennis Mallory." The smooth British accent blended perfectly with his warm smile. He extended his hand toward her as a sparkle quickly darted through his alert gray eyes and across his handsome features.

His gaze slowly traveled from her face, along each and every curve of her body, then back to her face. She had dressed in peach-colored silk slacks and a matching blouse, gold earrings, and the single gold chain she always wore around her neck, the same one Blaine had given her all those years ago. She had styled her long, blonde hair in an upswept manner away from her face.

He regained eye contact with her, placing his other hand over hers as they shook hands. "Please…please tell me you're Meg Wainwright."

A warm flush moved through her veins, a strong and unexpected physical reaction to Dennis that left her momentarily rattled and uneasy. She noted the stylish cut of his glossy, brown hair and the way his clothes perfectly fit his well-built six-foot frame, his suit obviously custom tailored and expensive, his silk necktie monogrammed.

Meg tendered a smile as she withdrew her hand from his very tempting grasp and stepped aside so he could enter the suite. "Yes, I'm Meg Wainwright. It's a pleasure to meet you." She crossed the room to the bar. The intensity of his gaze followed her, sending an odd tingling sensation up her spine. She turned to face him, extending a friendly smile. "May I offer you something to drink?"

"Yes, thank you. A whisky and water. That's scotch and water without ice, for the benefit of those who speak only American." His contagious smile and sparkling eyes teased.

She laughed, an open easy laugh that quickly alleviated the tension building inside her. "As someone once said, something about the British and Americans being one people separated by a common language. I think it might have been George Bernard Shaw with Churchill paraphrasing it when he spoke before our Congress during World War II."

"Ah, yes…both a quote and a misquote that have been around for quite a while. It's one of my favorites. It has been attributed to Oscar Wilde before Shaw. In 1887, Wilde wrote in *The Canterville Ghost*, 'We have really everything in common with America nowadays except, of course, language.' However, Shaw was quoted as saying, 'England and America are two countries separated by the same language.' Since the Wilde version actually exists in a book and definitely pre-dates Shaw and Churchill, I tend to go along with that."

"Well, you certainly seem to know your famous quotes."

He extended a charming smile. "One of the results of working in the publishing business."

She fixed his drink, handed it to him, and turned the conversation to business. "I'm very surprised at the expense you've gone to on my behalf. First class airfare, this beautiful suite in a luxury hotel rather than just a room in a more out-of-the-way extended stay hotel, limo service from the airport. Possibly appropriate for a multi-million, bestselling author, but this all seems very extravagant for a travel book."

"Don't worry about it, luv. Our publisher said everything was to be first class, so first class it is." He opened his portfolio case and covered the dining table with several layouts and sketches. "I suggest we move right to business. I'm sure you must be totally exhausted by now and would like to get some sleep, but I wanted to go over this with you tonight so you could give it some thought before our meeting in the morning."

"You prefer using the portfolio case rather than an electronic tablet to present the information?"

"Tablets are good for certain things, but I prefer old

school—being able to lay out large sheets of paper. They show everything in detail rather than needing to zoom in to get details on the tablet, therefore losing the overall image and taking the details out of context."

He quickly became all business as they discussed the book project and what the company wanted to achieve with the new line of travel books. He showed her how this specific book and the travel line in general would be laid out. They discussed the target audience, photo concepts, and copy direction. She would write the main narrative, taking the pictures and identifying the photographs. The actual picture captions as well as services listings such as accommodations, restaurants, and tourist attractions would be written by one of the staff assistant editors. After about two hours, they had covered the basics of what the book would contain and how it would be laid out.

Dennis picked up all of his papers and returned them to his case. "Well, luv, you must surely be beyond exhaustion by now." He gave Meg another appraising onceover. "I must say, though, you look as fresh as a new day."

She experienced a quiver of excitement when he leaned closer to her. His warm breath tickled across her cheek. "You smell divine. I don't know what that perfume is, but you should never stop using it."

Once again, she experienced the unsettling pull of his sexual magnetism. She took a step back as she nervously played with the gold chain around her neck. "Thank you. How nice of you to say so."

"Well, luv. It's time to call it a night. I'll send the limo for you tomorrow morning to bring you to the offices. Will half past ten be convenient for you?"

"Ten-thirty will be fine." She walked with him toward the front door of the suite. "The way you've presented the layout of this first book is very interesting. I think this is going to be an exciting project. I'm looking forward to getting started on it."

When they reached the door, he flashed a sexy smile as he held out a hand. "Well, it has indeed been a pleasure. I'll see you in the morning. Good night, luv." He leaned forward again as they shook hands and gave her a light kiss on the cheek before leaving.

Meg closed the door, then leaned back against it and took a deep breath. Dennis Mallory—an extremely attractive yet very disconcerting man. He certainly made no attempt to hide his desires and thoughts. She found the undeniable magnetic pull of his sexual energy a bit unnerving. She took another deep breath in an attempt to quell the nervous energy caused by his nearness, then walked toward the bedroom. It had been a very long day. Exhaustion ranked high on her list.

After undressing and washing off her makeup, she took a pair of pajamas from the dresser drawer, looked at them, shrugged, and put them back. Why had she even bothered to pack them? She preferred sleeping in the nude, a habit she had acquired during the time she and Blaine had been together. A sudden flood of sadness washed over her. Not only had they been together, but they had been in love.

Or so she had thought. As it turned out, she was the only one in love.

That had been ten years ago. For what seemed like the millionth time, she wondered if the emotional hurt would ever go away. She allowed her mind to briefly drift to the last time she had seen Blaine—had any contact with him—that horrible day ten years ago when he walked out of her life severing a relationship she thought would last forever. She shook away the painful memories, slid beneath the sheets, and sank into the softness of the bed.

She fell into a deep sleep, not stirring until the next morning when she stretched, wiggled her toes, slowly opened her eyes, and focused on the clock. She jerked to immediate attention. She had slept for ten straight hours. The limo would be at the hotel in another two hours. She quickly jumped out of bed and headed toward the shower.

At exactly ten-thirty, William pulled up in front of the hotel as she walked out the door. He expertly maneuvered the limo into the bustling streets of the Knightsbridge district and headed toward the offices of Pendragon Publishing. Ten minutes later, they arrived in front of an older building bearing the company name on a large brass plaque next to the door.

Caroline, the receptionist, greeted Meg as if they knew each other even though they had never met. "Good morning, Miss Wainwright. I'll notify Mr. Mallory that you're here."

Meg seated herself in a comfortable chair as she looked around the lobby. The interior design of the building appeared in sharp contrast to its old exterior. Light and airy with large expanses of open space provided a totally uncluttered look. Antique accessories combined with contemporary decor, mostly soft muted shades with occasional splashes of bright color. She noticed a profusion of green plants. Tapestries—some appeared old and others new—adorned the walls interspersed with large photographs depicting Pendragon book covers and authors. The overall effect presented an eclectic blend of antique and contemporary. Something about the style, the general tone and feel, seemed very familiar—uncomfortably familiar.

"Meg, luv, you look absolutely marvelous." Dennis stepped from the staircase and crossed the lobby as he smiled and extended his hand. "You must thrive on jet lag. One would never know you flew in from Los Angeles just yesterday afternoon." His impeccable attire included a fashionably cut custom-tailored suit and Gucci loafers. She felt the warmth of his touch, felt the unsettling excitement he transmitted to her as he cupped her elbow while guiding her toward the elevator. "We'll take the lift to my office."

Meg sat across the desk from Dennis as they engaged in casual conversation. He suddenly diverted his gaze toward his office door behind her. "Ah, here comes our intrepid publisher now."

She turned in her chair, anxious to meet the man responsible for the success of this young but very dynamic company.

Meg's heart skipped a beat and her breath froze in her lungs as Blaine Reeves strode confidently into the office. It had been ten years. An uncontrollable surge of a too-long pent-up desire raced through her body. A barely audible gasp escaped her throat. A feeling of joy danced inside her ever so briefly before being quickly replaced by ten years of pain, anger, and emotional turmoil. She narrowed her eyes on him.

Blaine halted in mid stride, struck breathless by the sight of her. It had been ten years. The beautiful twenty-two-year-old he once knew had blossomed into a stunning, sophisticated woman. He had difficulty comprehending how she could be even more beautiful than the memory he had carried for all these years.

His gaze devoured the delicate features of her face, her blonde hair swept up on her head, the small gold earrings, and the single gold chain around her neck, the one he had given her. The green color of her dress exactly matched her exquisite eyes, the style accentuating her slim waist and long legs.

It took all his control to keep from reaching out to touch her, pulling her into his arms, and smothering her with kisses. It took all his willpower to maintain his ground as the scent of her perfume wafted across his nostrils, causing them to flare slightly while evoking memories more profound than any others in his life. It had been a time of blissful contentment and a happiness he thought would never end.

Then he had totally destroyed the best thing that had ever happened to him. Every day since then had been just one more day to endure. And now he had a chance to recapture what he should never have walked away from. To Blaine's adoring eyes she did not look one day older than when he last saw her.

Something momentarily flickered in her eyes, but it became lost to her anger before he could read it.

"Meg, luv," Dennis' voice intruded into the moment. "I'd like to introduce our publisher, Blaine—"

"I already know *Mr. Reeves.*" Her sharp tone cut through the air like a knife. The muscles in her face tightened as her body stiffened.

Her voice contained a hard, cold edge as she hurled angry words at Blaine. "Is this your idea of a joke? Because if it is, it's definitely a sick one."

"This is certainly not a joke. The job is very real."

Blaine's words came out in direct contrast, a timbre soft and warm. "My company is coming out with a new line of travel books. I wanted the best for this project. That's why I hired you. I've followed your career and have been very impressed with your many accomplishments."

Her attitude remained cold in spite of his words of praise. Her facial muscles tensed as she clenched her jaw even tighter. "Do you really believe for one moment that I'd be willing to work for you?"

He leveled a steady gaze at her. "You do remember the contract you signed and the advance check you cashed, don't you?"

Blaine turned his attention to a confused looking Dennis. "Would you please excuse us?"

Dennis mustered a slight smile and left his own office, a perplexed expression on his face.

Blaine closed the door, then turned back to Meg. He reached out for her hand.

An incredible jolt of electricity jumped between them, a potent rush of emotion accompanied by an intense desire. She quickly yanked her hand away. A distinct look of trepidation crossed through her eyes as she nervously paced back and forth, all the while her fingers toying with the gold chain. Blaine watched her every move, anxiously waiting for her response.

She abruptly stopped pacing and turned toward him.

"Well, *Mr. Reeves*, you seem to have me legally boxed in." Her voice contained a strained mixture of anger and bitterness but not enough to cover the underlying pain. "If this job is legitimate, as you *claim*, then let's refrain from delving into all the personal reminiscences and confine our conversation to business. Otherwise, I intend to be on the next flight back to Los

Angeles, whatever the consequences."

He took a calming breath. What he had to do next would not be easy, but it had to be done. He had given it many hours of agonizing thought after receiving her signed contract guaranteeing her presence in London, carefully weighing the pros versus the cons. As much as the prospect pained him, he had to do it. He could not take a chance that she would somehow uncover the truth on her own. He needed to start with a clean slate of honesty. They could not have the future together that he so desperately wanted until the past had been cleared away. "First, I want to explain what happened ten years ago. You have the right to know."

"Save your breath. That's ancient history. It's no longer of any interest to me and definitely not relevant to my life. If you want to cleanse your conscience, find a therapist or unload your problems on a friendly bartender."

Meg spat the words as if they were poison, but more than anything she wanted to resolve the emotional distress, to banish the turmoil that had twisted inside her for ten years. She needed to put closure to this most painful event in her life.

She gave him a long hard look. "My contract calls for you to provide me with an assistant for transportation, to handle my photographic equipment, and run errands while we're on location. I'll expect whoever it is at my hotel Monday morning at seven o'clock so I can get started on the assignment. The sooner I begin, the sooner I can get out of here…and far away from you."

Blaine grabbed her wrist to prevent her from turning away. Her muscles tensed accompanied by a quick intake of breath. She tried to wrest her arm from his grasp, but he refused to let go. "Please, Meg. Listen to what I have to say."

She turned an expressionless mask toward him, then shot a long, hard look in his direction, her voice devoid of even a hint of warmth. "Very well. But there's nothing you can say that will change the past, and it definitely won't help the future or alter the distastefulness of this situation."

Blaine closed his eyes for just a moment as he gathered his determination before proceeding. He took in a steadying breath, held it for a second, then forced out the words he knew he needed to say. "We had been dating for almost a year when I met this woman. I was twenty-seven and she was forty-nine—attractive, quite sophisticated, worldly, and extremely wealthy. She praised my work as art director of the magazine and said I was much too talented to be wasting my time there. She claimed to have contacts in London and could get me on as managing editor with one of the magazines at a large British publishing house."

Anxiety edged into his voice as his carefully rehearsed words seemed to crumble faster than he could get them out of his mouth. With great difficulty, he pushed forward. "She totally seduced me with the prospect of wealth and power, flattered me into thinking I was the greatest lover she ever had—"

A shudder moved through her body at the mention of the word *lover*. Her eyes widened and filled with the most incredible hurt he had ever witnessed. The glimpse into her emotional pain lasted only a moment before her eyes narrowed and hardened into anger. But it had been long enough for it to totally permeate his reality. He took another calming breath before continuing. He knew he had set a difficult task for himself, but until that moment, he hadn't realized just how difficult.

"I was putty in her hands. I didn't seem to have any will of my own. She took me to London with her. All I could see was a very impressive position—wealth, success, international connections, the jet set life. In my mind's eye, I saw myself as the envy of everyone I came in contact with."

He paused and looked into her eyes. Her anger faded, replaced by the same deep hurt he had glimpsed earlier. He slowly forced out the words. "I behaved in a very immature and selfish manner. I was incredibly stupid." He reflected for a moment. "Crista told me I was a damn fool. I guess trying to knock some sense into their younger brothers is what older sisters do best."

He collected his thoughts, strengthened his resolve, and gathered together what he hoped would be the proper words. "Everything real, down-to-earth, and honest simply flew out the window, taking my integrity and ethics with it." He lowered his gaze, taking a moment to stare at the floor. "What happened next was no more than what I deserved. After two months, the job still hadn't come about. I finally got my head out of the clouds and realized she was just using me as a plaything to parade around on her arm. When I objected to what had been happening and pushed her toward providing the job she promised, she found herself an even younger boy toy and dumped me on the spot. For the next couple of months, I wandered around England supporting myself in various ways such as teaching tennis and using whatever artistic talent I have. All my thoughts centered on how in the world I'd ever be able to return to you, ever convince you to see me again. I had nothing to offer you. I didn't even have a steady job, and my future prospects looked bleak. I didn't have a prayer you'd even talk to me, considering my deplorable actions, let alone forgive me."

His voice quavered slightly. "I missed you so much—your softness, gentleness, intelligence, and honesty. I didn't stand a chance with you after what I'd done."

He returned to a matter-of-fact tone. "I decided to stay in London and work very hard to make a success of myself, on my own, so I would be able to offer you something and hope in time you would find it in your heart to forgive me. I've built my own publishing company. Through a combination of hard work and a lot of good luck, I've become very successful. With the launching of the travel book series, I was finally in a position to offer you an assignment, so I could get you to London."

He looked intently into her angry eyes. "I can only plead temporary insanity to explain my deplorable behavior and ask you to forgive me." His voice became almost a whisper as emotion choked him. "In retrospect, I think I was afraid of how close we'd become. Taking that final step, making a lifetime commitment, truly terrified me."

He breathed a sigh of relief, thankful that the difficult words had at last been spoken. "Now you have the entire sordid tale." He looked into her eyes. "The only thing that's given me the strength to accomplish what I have, the drive to continue when things seemed too bleak, was the hope that someday I would be able to share it with you."

Without saying a word, she wrenched her arm from his grasp and walked across the office. When she reached the door, she whirled around to face him, her anger and hurt lashing out in equal proportions. "You must have had quite a laugh at my expense. Naïve twenty-two-year-old Meg—not worldly, not sophisticated, and definitely not wealthy. I had nothing to offer—only my heart and my love."

Tears welled in Meg's eyes. She forced back the sob that formed in her throat. "Did you leave my bed and hurry directly to hers or was it the other way around?" The next words were out of her mouth before she could stop them, but she made no effort to soften her sarcasm. "Perhaps congratulations are in order. Such a splendid display of stamina."

He flinched as her words hit their mark. He opened his mouth to speak, but she held up a hand to stop him. "Don't bother. It doesn't matter." She shot a hard look in his direction. "I do have to thank you for one thing, though. You threw me full force into the world of reality. I learned a hard lesson, but I learned it well. The only person I can trust is me."

With that, she turned on her heel and stormed out of the office headed toward the elevator.

Blaine stood motionless in Dennis' office for a long moment, then allowed a sigh to escape his throat as he walked down the hall toward his own office.

He slowly shook his head as he muttered to no one in particular. "Well, I knew it wasn't going to be easy."

When he reached his office, Emily handed him several phone messages. "Mr. Reeves, your solicitor has been ringing you all morning. He seems most anxious to speak with you."

"Thanks, Emily. Get him on the phone for me, please." He continued across his office while looking through the stack of messages. The phone rang, and he quickly grabbed it. "Harry, what's so important?"

"We have problems with the most recent Sinclair proposal. The details have been leaked, just like last time."

Blaine's anger leaped across the phone lines. "How the hell are they finding out what I'm doing? We've been in negotiations with Sinclair for almost three months, and now, all of a sudden, my every move is known. The most recent proposal has only been in their hands for two days. None of my officers or department heads have had any involvement in this transaction. The leak must be from your office or from Wendell's office at the bank. Find out what's going on and stop it!"

Blaine slammed down the receiver, then slumped back in his chair. A quick jab of guilt assaulted his senses. There was no excuse for his harsh attitude with Harry. He was still upset over how badly things had gone with Meg and had allowed his frustration to carry over to an unrelated matter.

He picked up the phone and dialed his attorney's private number directly into his office. "Harry…sorry about that outburst. I have a personal situation that's not going well, and the unfortunate timing of your call had me taking it out on you."

"No problem. We all have those off days now and then."

He spoke with his attorney for another couple of minutes about an unrelated matter before terminating the call. Then he leaned back in his chair, his thoughts centering on Meg.

Emily interrupted his mood when she entered his office and handed him a cup of coffee. In her usual crisp, efficient manner, she addressed the business at hand. "Are we ready to respond to the post that has been accumulating since last Tuesday?"

Blaine gave her a weary sigh. "I guess we're ready to respond." Blaine sipped his coffee as Emily returned to her desk to get her steno pad. She represented the perfect stereotype of a prim spinster—her sensible shoes, bland business suit, and mousy brown hair worn in a tight bun at the back of her head with the wisps of gray showing throughout.

Although a little too up tight and aloof in her attitude for Blaine's personal taste, she was without a doubt the most efficient secretary he ever had. He guessed her age to be around fifty. She had never been married, still lived with her parents, and probably had a non-existent social life. However, lately she had been getting personal phone calls and just that morning someone sent her flowers.

Blaine smiled. Maybe Emily had finally found a nice gentleman companion. He dismissed the idle thought and returned his attention to the leak of information about his current negotiations.

Chapter Two

Meg hailed a cab to take her back to the hotel. When she reached the suite, she angrily kicked off her shoes and fixed herself a stiff drink. As she sipped her scotch and water, her anger subsided, replaced by an overwhelming rush of unwanted feelings and thoughts from the past.

An aching emptiness washed over her, the same emptiness that continually lived deep inside her—a loneliness in her heart. She had experienced other lovers over the last ten years, primarily in an attempt to forget Blaine. Every man she met had been compared to Blaine, and all had been found lacking. Could ten years of hurt and longing be swept away by a quick explanation? And more importantly, would she ever be able to trust him again, especially now that she knew about the other woman and what had really happened?

She had been a long time healing. Did she dare allow him back into her life? Become vulnerable? Put herself in a position where all the old wounds could be ripped open? Where he could hurt her all over again? She shook her head in a moment of realization. Correction—all the old wounds had already been ripped open.

Her mind drifted. Vivid memories. His smell, his taste, his touch. She took a calming breath. An almost uncontrollable flood of emotion settled over her as she recalled how they had met and the first time they made love. He had been the art director at the magazine where she had been hired for a freelance photography assignment. To her delight, once the assignment ended and their business relationship concluded, he'd asked her out to dinner.

They had been dating for almost two months, during which time she had resisted his numerous sexual advances. Then they had gone on a picnic. He had selected a beautiful green meadow dotted with colorful wildflowers next to a clear rushing stream. The warm sunlight filtered through the trees while a gentle breeze seductively rustled the leaves. It felt as if they were the only two people in the world.

He had put his arms around her and gently laid her on the blanket, brushing his lips softly against hers before his kiss deepened. She knew making love with Blaine would be very different from what she had experienced. The kiss became more passionate. There was nothing subtle about the smoldering fire that had immediately singed her nerve endings. She had experienced sensations she had never before known. He started to unbutton her blouse, but she had asked him not to go any farther.

She had started to say she was sorry. She didn't want him to think she was just leading him on. He had put his fingertips to her mouth to hush her words. Kissing her lightly on the lips again, he told her he very much wanted to make love to her, but not if she felt uncomfortable about it. She had looked into his eyes and knew at that moment how very much she loved Blaine Reeves.

He had leaned forward and kissed her, at first gently nibbling at her lips, then with more fervor. He held her close and whispered in her ear, "Don't be afraid, Meg. I won't hurt you. I'd never do anything to hurt you."

The memory of Blaine's whispered words snapped Meg back to the present. He had hurt her. Not physically, but most assuredly emotionally. He hurt her more than she thought possible. How she had loved him, trusted him, believed in him, and in the future she thought they would share. And now, suddenly, he reappeared in her life wanting her to forgive him and trust him again as if nothing had happened. To simply forget the last ten years, cast off the horrible pain, and start all over again. To *trust* him.

The years had truly enhanced his desirability. Unexpected waves of yearning swept through her body the moment he had grabbed her wrist. After all those years, all it took was one touch and her resolve immediately started to crumble. And now, all she wanted was to get through this assignment and return home where she could feel safe again.

Safe—the word conjured up that night long ago at his apartment. She had felt so safe as he wrapped her in the protection of his arms. He had said he would never hurt her, and she had believed him. Her sensual desires and overwhelming love for Blaine had eclipsed her fears. She had tentatively lifted her mouth to his and kissed him softly. Her words had come out in a trembling voice barely above a whisper. "Make love to me."

He had elevated her to heights of ecstasy beyond anything she had ever imagined. In her wildest fantasies, she had never dreamed it could be so enthralling. He had been gentle, caring, and patient.

Meg shook her head to rid her mind of the unwelcome memories, but she could not quell the physical excitement coursing through her veins. She gathered her determination. His betrayal from the past could not be changed. The good times could not be recaptured nor could those memories erase the hurt of that terrible night when he had walked out and disappeared from her life for ten long years. She needed to put it all behind her and move forward to the future. As much as the memory of their lovemaking fueled her desires, Blaine Reeves did not represent her future. He was bad for her in every way, a reality he had proven ten years ago.

She slowly swirled the ice cubes and watched them come to rest at the bottom of her glass. The words she had been desperately trying to ignore finally forced their way to her lips. The sound of her own voice shattered the stillness of the room.

"I know I'll never be able to trust you again, and it would be foolish of me to think we could have a future together, but I've ached for you every night for ten years and yearned for you every day. God help me, I still love you, Blaine."

****

"This way, gentlemen." Emily showed Harry and Wendell into Blaine's office then left, closing the door behind her. The three men sat at the small conference table. They spread out papers and legal documents.

Blaine took command of the meeting. "Harry, are you making any headway on this information leak?"

"I've not been able to discover anything about our problem. All my associates swear they've told no one about these dealings."

Wendell agreed with Harry. "No one at the bank has any idea how the information is getting out. I'm sorry, Blaine. I can't think of where else to check."

Blaine looked from his attorney to his banker. "I may have to end up putting a private detective on it." He emitted an amused chuckle. "I wonder if Sherlock Holmes is available." Then his expression turned serious again. "In the meantime, let's get down to today's business. Let me see the completed restructuring of the newest proposal." Harry handed Blaine a legal document. Blaine read the pages making notations as he went, then set it on the table. "This looks good, Harry, just a few minor changes. Wendell, have you gone over these figures?"

"Yes, I have. They're solid. It's a very fair offer to Sinclair and a financially good move for you. Here's the latest financials."

Blaine looked over the profit and loss statements. "Okay, gentlemen. Let's do this one." Blaine walked to the door and opened it. "Emily, would you make these indicated changes and have the documents hand delivered to Sinclair's attorney before the close of business today?"

"Certainly, Mr. Reeves. I will attend to it straight away." Emily took the papers and returned to her desk as her phone rang. Her austere features softened, a smile turned the corners of her thin lips, and her voice lowered.

"Robert, how good to hear from you. Yes, I received the flowers. They're lovely." She leaned forward to inhale the fragrance of the attractive arrangement on the corner of her desk. "Why, yes, I would be delighted to have dinner with you this evening. Of course, that would be perfect. Half past six. I look forward to seeing you then."

She disconnected from the call, lingering a moment with her hand still on the receiver. Blaine's office door opened behind her, startling her out of her brief moment of reflection. She immediately resumed her work.

Blaine escorted Harry and Wendell out of his office. "Hopefully this will do it. We should have some kind of response from Sinclair by the end of next week. Gentlemen, have a good weekend."

Blaine shook hands with the two men as they left his office. He turned his attention to Emily. "How are you coming with the documents? They need to be to Sinclair's attorney by four-thirty this afternoon. Are we going to make it?"

Her normally austere manner returned. "Of course, Mr. Reeves. The documents will be at their destination on schedule."

Blaine returned to his office. He took care of some paperwork, had a meeting with the art department, then phoned Meg at her hotel. After four rings, she finally answered.

"Hi." Blaine maintained an open warmth to his voice. "I was about to hang up. Did I catch you at a bad time?"

"I just came back from a jog in Hyde Park. I heard the phone ringing as I opened the door."

"I wanted to call earlier, but I've been tied up in meetings all afternoon. Let's have dinner tonight."

"I would have given you the same answer if you had called earlier," she replied, cold and distant. "The answer is no. I see no reason for us to socialize. Goodbye."

Without giving him a chance to reply, she quickly hung up leaving him staring at a dead phone. He gathered his determination. *I knew it wouldn't be easy.* He turned off his office light on the way out.

Emily looked up from her desk as he closed his

office door. "Good night, Mr. Reeves."

"Good night, Emily. Have a nice weekend."

"Oh, I will. I have a dinner engagement this evening." She smiled, a glow of anticipation on her face.

It warmed him to know she really had found someone. He headed toward the stairs. He knew all about loneliness and what a lousy place it could be.

Emily gathered her purse, locked her desk, turned out her light, and hurried home to prepare for her date. She was ready when the impeccably dressed, distinguished-looking man in his early fifties with dark hair graying at the temples arrived to pick her up. They drove to an elegant restaurant where they were seated immediately.

Emily and Robert enjoyed a superb dinner. After the waiter cleared the dishes from the table, Robert filled her wine glass then replenished his own. Her words gushed in a non-stop flow. "Oh, my. Not another glass. This will be two glasses. I'm not accustomed to drinking this much."

She giggled slightly as she took another sip. "This is such a nice restaurant—the china, silver, crystal, candlelight, and the music." Her gaze traveled around the room, taking in all the details. "I've never been in such an elegant establishment." She sipped her wine and giggled again as she tried to hold back a hiccup. "Oh, my. Please excuse me, Robert. This is more than I am accustomed to drinking. My usual consumption is an occasional glass of sherry with mother and father in the evening."

The crimson warmth spread across her face and neck as the wine loosened her prim manner.

Robert smiled solicitously. "I'm very pleased that

you like the restaurant. I travel so much with my sales job, one night here and one night there, that I seldom have the opportunity to leisurely dine in nice restaurants like this. I'm so glad you were able to join me tonight, especially on such short notice. I had an evening appointment in Windsor, but it cancelled at the last minute. I took a chance you would be able to dine with me and hurried back home."

"You know, Robert, I don't recall what it is you sell. What company do you work for?"

He chuckled as he projected a casual manner. "I sell frames for eyeglasses. Really, my job is very dull." He paused as he took another sip of his wine. "You, on the other hand, have a very interesting job working for a publisher. You've told me a little about what you do, but I'd really like to hear more. You make it sound very exciting." He slowly refilled her wine glass as he paused in his subtle questioning, then he signaled the waiter.

"Yes, sir. Will there be something else?"

"We'd like to see the sweet trolley, please." The waiter left and immediately returned with the dessert cart. Robert deferred to Emily. "What would you like?"

"Oh, my. Everything looks so delicious. I really shouldn't be doing this." She pointed toward a pastry. "I'd like this one." The waiter placed the dessert on a plate and set it in front of her.

"And you, sir?"

"I'll have the same."

"Very good, sir." The waiter placed the item in front of Robert, then took the cart away.

Emily gushed her words, her speech slightly slurred from the wine. "I really should not be eating this…all of these calories."

"Why, Emily. You have a lovely figure. There's no reason for you to be concerned."

She shyly dropped her gaze to the dessert plate in front of her.

"I'm sorry, Emily. I didn't mean to embarrass you." He offered a confidence inducing smile. "Forgive me?"

She looked up at him and smiled. "Do you…do you really think so?" Too many factors played on her senses. A combination of the wine, the unaccustomed attentions from a man, and the heady swirl of compliments.

"I wouldn't have said so if I didn't think it was true." His warm voice soothed her concerns. She giggled and took another sip of her wine. He raised his glass toward her in a toast. "To you and many more evenings like tonight."

Again, she felt the heat of embarrassment flush across her cheeks as they each sipped their wine.

He set his glass on the table. "You were going to tell me about the interesting things that happen on your job." His expression brightened, as if a sudden thought had just occurred to him. "I know, you tell me about your activities for today, and I'll share with you how I spent my time." He looked at her, smiling attentively as she began to talk.

"Well…" Her brow wrinkled in concentration for a moment. "I believe I mentioned the negotiations that Mr. Reeves is currently engaged in. It's all very confidential, especially now. There has been some kind of information leak about what has been happening. Mr. Reeves thinks it's from either the solicitor's office or the bank."

Robert reached across the table and covered her hand with his, encouraging her to continue.

Across the room, Dennis Mallory entered the

restaurant in the company of a stunning brunette, one of several such beautiful women who were constantly seen in the most fashionable places as his companion of the evening. As he looked around the room, his gaze landed on Emily having an intimate dinner with a man. Surprise and confusion entered his mind simultaneously. This certainly wasn't the type of place he would expect to see Emily. Not dowdy, spinsterish Emily. He continued to stare at them. There was something familiar about the man, but he couldn't quite place him.

His date pressed her body suggestively against his, capturing his full attention. She whispered in his ear. He turned his head toward her and extended a sexy smile as his thoughts dismissed Emily and her date. Pure lust coursed through his veins.

"Luv, this will certainly be the quickest dinner in history, then it's back to your flat." He sent one last troubled glance toward Emily as the maître d' took them to their table.

****

Meg lingered in bed Saturday morning after waking. She enjoyed the first lazy moments of the day—the feel of the soft sheets against her bare skin, the fact that she didn't have to get up, didn't need to be anywhere. The jarring intrusion of the phone forced her eyes open.

"Good morning. I hope I didn't wake you." Blaine's soft, mellifluous voice sent a slight shiver through her body. Her breathing quickened.

She forced her words, thick with irritation due as much to the desires she couldn't turn off as to the sound of his voice or the early hour of his phone call. "It's seven o'clock in the morning, Blaine. What do you want?"

"I want you to have breakfast with me. After that,

we can take a boat ride on the Thames or play some tennis. It's a beautiful, sunny day, and we should take advantage of it."

"I thought I made myself very clear yesterday. I see no reason for us to socialize. As you so succinctly pointed out, you have a signed contract for my professional services. I'm here on business, albeit through your subterfuge, and that's the end of it."

"Okay, then how about dinner tonight?"

She moved from irritation to anger. "You're not listening to me. I said no. No dinner, no breakfast, no socializing. No."

"What would you think about brunch tomorrow?"

"Blaine!" An involuntary chuckle escaped her throat before she could contain it.

"Well, so you can still laugh. Now, back to my question. Is there some meal we can eat together this weekend? Any meal you say."

"No. I'm quite serious. This is strictly business. There will be no socializing. Don't ask again. Goodbye, Blaine."

She hung up the phone, let out a growl of exasperation, kicked her feet against the mattress, then pulled the covers over her head. But the childish action didn't help. She was now wide awake. No way could she go back to sleep.

Blaine had been right about one thing. A nice sunny day shouldn't be wasted. She climbed out of bed, made a quick trip through the shower, and dressed casually with comfortable walking shoes. It would be a good day for sightseeing, perhaps one of those half-day tours of the city followed by some shopping. Or maybe a river trip on the Thames to Greenwich and a tour of the observatory. She grabbed her purse and a map of the London Underground. She would put Blaine Reeves out of her mind and enjoy her free weekend before going to work on Monday.

She started down the street and got as far as the underground station when she noticed Harrods in the next block. She had made her decision. A few minutes later, she pushed through the doors of the venerable old establishment and entered a shopper's paradise—everything from the common to the unusual to the extreme and the most luxurious.

Meg didn't return to the hotel until late afternoon. She kicked off her shoes, set her packages on the dining table, then immediately sank into the couch. She had spent the entire day covering every square inch of Harrods and now wanted nothing more than to order dinner from room service and stay in.

****

Dennis, on the other hand, had no such mundane evening planned for himself. Saturday night found him and his date, a redhead every bit as stunning as the previous night's brunette, lingering over an after-dinner drink in a fashionable West End restaurant. A very subtle flash of anticipation and excitement darted through him as his date slipped her hand under the table and seductively ran her long, lacquered fingernails across his thigh. But when he turned to signal the waiter to bring the check, his attention became riveted on a table across the room.

The man he had seen with Emily last night was involved in an obviously intense conversation over dinner with two other men. Dennis immediately recognized one of the men as Sir Geoffrey Lewiston, the powerful head of one of Britain's largest publishing houses. Then he recalled the name of Emily's date—Robert Templeton, Sir Geoffrey's right-hand man in charge of whatever underhanded or unethical things Sir Geoffrey needed done.

What would Emily be doing with Robert Templeton? What could they possibly have in common? A very puzzling situation, indeed.

His date interrupted his thoughts when she whispered in his ear. He immediately turned his attention to her. "Yes, luv, it's surely time to move on to other things. We'll go to your flat."

He gave one last glance at the three men. Emily and Robert Templeton being together bothered him. It didn't make any sense.

It looked like trouble.

****

Meg woke early Sunday morning and prepared to go for a jog in Hyde Park. Jogging always helped clear her head and set her on the right path when she had to deal with something troubling. She knew an immediate feeling of calm would settle over her as the emotional confusion cleared from her head and logic took control. Her contract with Pendragon Publishing gave her a lucrative assignment and outstanding credit for her résumé. She was a mature professional and could separate personal from business. Besides, she would be away from the office photographing around London for the next few days, then in the countryside for a few weeks finishing the assignment. There wouldn't really be any direct contact with Blaine.

Dressed in her running clothes with her hair pulled back in a ponytail, she had just put on a touch of lipstick when she heard a knock. She opened the door and found herself staring at Blaine's dazzling smile, at the dimples his smile brought out of hiding, and his incredibly handsome features.

His intoxicating nearness sent her heart pounding. Surely, he had to hear it. She inhaled the familiar scent she had always associated with him, the special aftershave he always wore mingled with his clean, masculine scent. She fought the almost unbearable need to reach out and touch his face, to run her finger along the scar on his chin. She had been in such a state of shock at seeing him Friday that her mind had been incapable of taking in all of the little nuances so particularly Blaine.

She gathered her determination, glared at him, and refused to step aside so he could enter the suite. "What are you doing here?"

He continued to rain his dazzling smile across her as he spoke in a soft, sexy tone that never failed to pull her in. "Don't I even rate a good morning?"

Her breathing quickened along with her pulse rate. "All right then, good morning." She fixed him with a hard stare. "Now, what are you doing here?"

"I came to take you to breakfast, then out for a day of whatever you would like to do. Are you ready to go?"

"I told you on the phone yesterday morning I'm not interested in having breakfast or any meal with you. I don't want to spend the day with you." She heard the faltering timbre creep into her voice. "Please…go away."

He looked into her eyes. "Meg, you can't continue to avoid me indefinitely. We have to talk about this."

"We have nothing to talk about." The pain welled inside her. "You made your decision ten years ago. You made it clear where you stood and what you wanted. You killed everything that existed between us. That relationship, or whatever it was, is dead and over."

She tried to close the door, but he quickly reached his hand out and shoved it all the way open.

"Please, Blaine. Go away."

He studied her for a moment. "This isn't over, Meg." He pulled her body to him and covered her mouth with his, a kiss filled with the passion and longing churning inside him. Her body stiffened. She put her hands against his chest and pushed as she turned her face away.

He released her. "It will never be over."

He reached out to touch her cheek, but she deftly moved out of his reach. "You're wrong. It's as dead and over now as it was when you walked out." She quickly shut the door, foiling any further advances or conversation.

Meg leaned back against the closed door. Her heart pounded, her senses wildly alive. She looked down at her trembling hands and experienced a sudden weakness in her legs. She blinked several times to drive away the tears that filled her eyes. How could she be feeling like this after what he had done to her? How was it possible for her to want him so much?

To still be so deeply in love with Blaine Reeves?

****

The Victoria and Albert Museum prepared to close late Sunday afternoon as Meg emerged from the building onto Cromwell Road. She raised her hand to hail a taxi. The sound of squealing tires and someone calling her name grabbed her attention. The sleek new sports car screeched to a halt at the curb.

Dennis reached across to the passenger side and opened the car door. "Meg, luv, what a surprise. Get in. I'll give you a lift."

"Dennis." She offered him a grateful smile. "Thanks, I'd love a ride." She slid into the car seat and closed the door. "I'm going back to my hotel if it's not out of your way."

"It's not out of my way at all, luv." He pulled away from the curb into the flow of traffic. "I'm a bit surprised to see you here. I assumed you would be out with Blaine."

Her body tensed with anxiety. "No, there's no reason why I would be with Blaine."

"Well, tell me, luv. How have you been spending your weekend? If I had known you were going to be all alone, I would certainly have taken you to dinner."

"How nice of you. Actually, I spent yesterday devouring every inch of Harrods. This morning I jogged in Hyde Park, and this afternoon, I took in the Victoria and Albert Museum. It was a very relaxing weekend. I needed the rest. I want to be fresh for tomorrow. It's the first day of shooting."

He pulled his car up in front of her hotel. "Here you are, a palace fit for a princess." He edged a little closer. "I have an engagement for later this evening, but I would be honored if you would allow me to buy you a drink now. May I?" He flashed one of his practiced sexy smiles.

She hesitated a moment, then spoke. "Sure, that would be nice."

They entered the hotel and went to the bar on the opposite side of the lobby.

"Here, luv, how about this nice quiet spot in the

corner?" He stood aside, allowing her to slide into the booth, then seated himself next to her rather than sitting across the table.

"I'm most anxious to see the photos you'll be shooting. Blaine told me how talented you are. I must apologize for not being personally familiar with your work. This entire project came about so suddenly and was presented to me as a completed deal—signed, sealed, and officially contracted before I was aware of anything beyond his early-stage planning of publishing a line of travel books. I'm afraid I didn't have time to properly do my research before your arrival."

She twirled the stem of her wine glass between her thumb and fingers. "Did Blaine mention that he and I had worked together on a magazine project ten years ago in Los Angeles?"

"No, he didn't tell me. He did give me a verbal rundown on your credentials. I must admit, I was very impressed. He recommends your work very highly."

She emitted an amused chuckle, albeit a slightly strained one. "And, since he's the boss, here you are…stuck with me."

"Meg, luv. How can you say that? I'm certainly not *stuck* with you. In fact"—he lowered his voice, giving his words a purposely sensual feel—"when we first met, I knew I wanted to know you better." He took a sip of his drink. "Tell me, luv. Are you married, engaged, or otherwise personally involved?"

A bittersweet laugh escaped her lips. "No, I'm none of the above."

"Well, that certainly doesn't speak very well for American men. You are a very desirable woman. Someone should have laid claim to you a long time ago."

Meg experienced a momentary flicker of irritation at the sexist connotation of someone *claiming* her as if she were a parcel to be picked up at the post office. But she quickly dismissed it, deferring to the light mood of the conversation. She extended a teasing grin. "I'll bet you say that to all the female freelancers who are foisted on you without your approval or acceptance."

He expressed a joking attitude, one indicating he had been grievously injured that she would assume such a thing. "You were hardly *foisted* on me. Had I been unhappy about the situation, I would simply have assigned one of my editors to work with you." His manner turned serious. "Tell me about your family—any brothers or sisters?"

"No, I was an only child." A moment of sadness slowly seeped into her reality. "My Mother died four years ago. My father died six months later, more from grief and a broken heart than anything else."

A forlorn look fleetingly darted across Dennis' face as he reached out and touched her cheek. "How fortunate you are to have been raised in a home of closeness with so much love and devotion."

His gaze stayed on her face for a moment longer, then he quickly returned to his upbeat manner, the persona that seemed to come naturally to him, as he flashed his sexy smile. "If you would like to have dinner tonight, I can cancel my previous engagement. We would have the entire evening, luv."

"Well, it's a tempting offer. But if I were the lady you had the date with, I'd be very unhappy if you cancelled out on me at the last minute like this, especially for no reason other than you found something you decided you'd rather do."

"As you Americans say, may I have a rain check?"

"It would be my pleasure." She looked at her watch. "But for now, we'd better call it an evening. Thanks for the drink."

Dennis walked her to the elevator. He leaned his face into hers, hesitated a moment, then placed an innocent kiss on her cheek. "Good night, luv."

An odd feeling swept through her as she rode up in the elevator. Something about Dennis, something very alluring yet equally troubling, and it left her uneasy.

Chapter Three

Meg woke at five-thirty Monday morning, anxious to start on her assignment. She quickly showered, then made coffee and poured some orange juice from the carton she had placed in the bar refrigerator. She opened the package of cinnamon rolls. While waiting for the coffee to brew, she dressed for her first day of location shooting.

After finishing her breakfast, she went through her equipment again. She cleaned filters and lenses, packed her collapsible reflector discs and stands along with two auxiliary flash units, double checked to make sure the batteries in cameras and flash units were fully charged, and accounted for all the items that should be in her gadget bag to verify she had everything she needed. She set her photo gear on her equipment cart next to the front door of the suite, ready to go. She glanced at the clock. Fifteen minutes before her assistant was due, just enough time to quickly scan the morning newspaper.

At precisely seven o'clock, she heard a knock at the door. As soon as she opened it, her eyes narrowed. A combination of surprise and anger jittered through her. "Why are you here again? I told you, no socializing."

Blaine smiled at her. "And again, no *good morning*? May I come in?"

She hesitated briefly before answering. "I suppose so, but only for a moment. My assistant will be here any minute, then I'm off to work." She stepped aside to let him in, making sure to maintain a safe distance from his way too tempting presence, a sensual aura difficult to ignore.

He quickly surveyed the room and spotted her cart. A barely audible sigh of resignation escaped his throat. "I had forgotten how much equipment went on a location shoot." He walked over to the cart, then turned to her with a confident smile. "Shall we go?"

"What are you talking about?"

He crossed the room toward her, his nearness causing her skin to tingle and her breathing to quicken. She took a step back.

"You said no meals and no socializing, so I decided the only way to spend time with you was to be your assistant. Now, we're not socializing." He shot her a mischievous grin, indicating his pleasure at the way he had manipulated the circumstances. "We're working."

"Very well. If the owner of the company has nothing better to do with his time than carry my equipment and run errands for me, so be it." She walked toward the door, her entire manner totally business. "Grab the cart, Blaine. Let's go."

His uncomfortable closeness as they rode down in the elevator stirred so many memories. She was thankful for the presence of other people. When they reached the front of the hotel, he loaded her equipment into the trunk of his car.

He effortlessly situated his tall frame behind the wheel then glanced over at her. "Where to?"

"Victoria Station. I want to catch people using all possible forms of public transportation. Victoria Station will give me the traditional double-decker red buses, motor coaches, the underground, Brit Rail, and the famous black-square London taxis waiting to pick up fares. It's also close to the hotel."

He smiled. "Your wish is my command." He started the car and pulled out into the morning traffic. "Did you have a nice weekend?"

"Yes."

He gave her a sideways glance and a wry smile. "Well, I guess this isn't a good time. We can chat later, perhaps over some lunch."

"I told you—"

"Please, Meg." A hint of mock indignation covered his face and surrounded his words. "We're out on location. We're working. We have to eat. It's a business lunch."

She looked at him. His expression indicated his integrity had been wounded beyond repair, the only giveaway being the twinkle in his blue eyes.

She slowly shook her head while trying to prevent the unwanted smile from turning up the corners of her mouth. She let out a sigh of resignation. "Blaine, Blaine, Blaine—what am I going to do with you?"

A sly grin tugged at his lips. "I have several suggestions."

She shot him a harsh look. "Don't push your luck."

He expertly maneuvered his car into a parking space outside Victoria Station and unloaded the camera equipment while she surveyed the scene, selecting her shots. People entering and exiting the station, the long line of identical square black taxis waiting for customers, the buses coming and going.

"Okay Meg, where do you want to start? The underground, buses, coaches, or trains?"

"Let's start indoors with the trains and the inside of the station in general."

The cavernous interior of Victoria Station with its bright skylights, numerous little shops, and food stands immediately engulfed her as she stepped inside. The constant bustle of people with suitcases heading to and from the train platforms perfectly suited the surroundings. She spent the morning shooting in and around Victoria Station with Blaine acting as her assistant, carrying her equipment and running general errands. The session went along smoothly.

Wary of his presence at first, she soon relaxed and immersed herself in the excitement of her work. Every now and then, she caught him staring at her with a look that made her uncomfortable.

"I think that about does it for this location." Meg put the cap on the camera lens. "Let's pack up and go."

He looked at his watch as he started to pack the equipment. "It's almost eleven-thirty. How about breaking for lunch? There's a pretty good Italian place a couple of blocks from here. How does Italian food sound to you?" She started to speak, but he stopped her. "Remember, this is strictly a business lunch."

She allowed a slight smile. "Right…strictly business." Then her manner brightened. "Italian sounds fine, and I am hungry. I only had coffee, juice, and a cinnamon roll for breakfast."

They were seated in the small restaurant. The aroma of cheeses, garlic, and various spices filled the air. The tables were covered with the traditional red and white checkered cloths. Waiters hurried back and forth taking orders and carrying trays of food.

Blaine ordered wine while Meg looked over the

menu. "What's your pleasure?"

"Everything looks and smells great." She closed the menu after making her selection. "I think I'll have the ravioli."

The waiter brought two glasses of wine then took their lunch order.

Blaine turned his attention to Meg again. "Excuse me for a minute. I need to check in with the office."

She watched him walk outside the restaurant as he pulled his cell phone from his pocket. His smooth, strong movements radiated self-confidence, a man sure of his place in the world. His appearance seemed tailored and impressive even though he wore jeans and a sweater. Once again, memories flooded her mind—the most recent one being the brief kiss from yesterday— memories that fed into her desire and her need for Blaine. She could still feel that brief moment of his mouth on hers—

She quickly forced the unwanted memories from her mind and turned her attention out the window to Blaine standing in front of the restaurant talking on his cell phone.

****

"Emily, it's me. What's going on?"

"Mr. Reeves, your solicitor has been desperate to contact you. I suggest you ring him immediately. I tried to contact you on your mobile phone, but the call went to your voice mail."

"I've had my phone turned off while we're working. Meg and I are having a quick lunch, then we're going over to Westminster Pier. I'll check in with you later this afternoon. I'll give Harry a call right now."

He dialed another number. "Harry…what's up?"

"Once again, our most recent proposal to Sinclair has been somehow intercepted, the one you just sent to them. It's like the information was compromised almost before it got to Sinclair's attorneys."

"How the hell are they finding out? This has to stop. I'll talk to you later." He disconnected from the call then paused to compose his thoughts before returning to the table and Meg.

"Is everything okay at the office? You look like someone dropped a bomb on you."

"What?" Blaine shook off the distraction of his phone conversation with Harry. "Oh, yeah…everything is fine. Just a minor problem I need to deal with later this afternoon." He took a swallow from his wine glass as the waiter served lunch.

"I think I shot some good pictures this morning. In fact, we're moving along faster than I thought we would. At this rate, I should be finished with all the planned London locations by the end of this week, then I can start on the countryside." She glanced at her watch. "I think we should be through by four o'clock today."

He moved closer to Meg, reaching out for her hand. She quickly withdrew from his reach and scooted away from him.

A warning note of caution surged through Meg's consciousness telling her to stay away from any physical contact with him. "This is strictly business, remember? It's a contracted work assignment, nothing more."

He looked into her eyes in an open and honest manner. "I mean to have you back as part of my life and will do whatever it takes to regain your trust."

His unwavering gaze sent a sudden rush of discomfort through her body. Confusion and uncertainty churned inside her, forcing her to look away. When she looked back, she once again hid herself behind the façade of icy indifference she had perfected. "Trust?" She spit out the word as if it was poison. "I'm surprised you don't choke on the concept."

They finished their lunch in silence, then moved on to the next photo location. She finished shooting around Westminster pier, including exterior shots of Parliament, Westminster Abbey, Horse Guards, and Whitehall. Blaine packed her equipment back in the car. The atmosphere between them continued to be strained. A great sense of relief settled over her now that the workday had finally come to an end.

Blaine pulled the car up in front of the hotel, took her equipment out of the trunk, and followed her to the front desk. The clerk handed her an envelope. Meg opened it and read the hand-written note on personalized stationery. A hint of a smile turned the corners of her mouth as she slipped it into her pocket. They took the elevator to her suite. After leaving her equipment cart by the door, he casually strolled over to the bar.

"You don't have time to fix yourself a drink. I won't be requiring your services as my assistant anymore today."

A quick flash of surprise darted across his face. "I thought we might have dinner." He flashed a dazzling smile causing his dimples to appear. "After all, it's still a workday."

"The workday ended five minutes ago. Besides"—a self-satisfied grin came to her lips—"I already have a dinner engagement for this evening."

His smile faded as his face registered disbelief. "I didn't think you knew anyone in London."

She allowed a hint of triumph to creep into her voice. "Ten years is a long time. There're lots of things you don't know about me."

He quickly closed the distance between them. His nearness took her breath away. His touch, his caress, his kiss. The flood of memories washed over her. No, she could not allow him to do this to her again, to turn her life upside down more than he already had with his under-handed ploy of an enticing work assignment.

She turned her icy stare on him. "You'd better leave so I can get ready for my dinner engagement."

In spite of her concentrated effort, her tone didn't quite match her projected exterior of indifference. She saw it—the flicker of heated intensity in his eyes—but could not move fast enough to avoid his sudden aggression. He swept her into his arms, covering her startled mouth with his.

She tried to push him away as his strong arms held her in a tight embrace. Her heart pounded as he pulled her against his hard chest. Her mind screamed no, but her desires betrayed her with a resounding yes. Slowly, she succumbed to his kiss as she reached her arms around his neck. She experienced the fire of his passion as their tongues touched and twined. A thousand emotions and memories flooded through her.

Then reason prevailed. She quickly broke away from his sensual mouth and all too tantalizing touch.

Blaine grabbed Meg by the shoulders, preventing her from turning away. He saw it in her eyes, a confused mixture of frightened girl and passionate woman. Her eyes frantically searched his face for some kind of a sign.

He squeezed his fingers into her upper arms, only vaguely aware of how tightly he held her. "You can't tell me you don't still feel something for me." His voice barely rose above a whisper. "I tasted it in your kiss. This is definitely not over. It will never be over."

He released her from his tight grip and quickly departed, leaving her standing motionless in the middle of the room. He stood with his back pressed against the corridor wall outside Meg's suite—his eyes closed, his head bent forward, and his open palms pressed firmly against his hard thighs. How he had missed her. How he wanted her.

But his passions were quickly taking control over his logic and common sense—his need to be with her, his intense love for her, the over-whelming emotion that had never died.

She still felt something for him, in spite of her words and the cold façade she tried to project. He tasted the earthiness of her kiss, the fire of her lips, felt her trembling body pressed against his, her resistance draining away. He still had a chance with her, and he would not let it slip away. As much as he wanted to carry her into the bedroom and spend the entire night making love, he needed to proceed carefully. The door had opened, albeit only a sliver. He had to make sure she wouldn't slam it shut again.

He gave one last glance of longing at her door, then slowly headed toward the elevator.

****

Meg remained frozen to the spot as she stared at the closed door, the one where Blaine had just departed. Her trembling fingers rested lightly on her lips. She felt the familiar scorching sensations he had always been able to call forth with only the slightest of touches, the fiery demands of his burning lips, the breathless ecstasy of his kiss.

And the one thing she could not afford to acknowledge, the one reality she dared not allow to exist—how much she still loved him.

She stumbled to the couch and sat for several minutes lost in thought, confused, and shaken. That kiss should not have happened, and she had to make sure it never happened again. No one would ever be allowed to hurt her the way Blaine had, and she would never allow herself to be in a position where he could do it again. She walked to the phone.

"Dennis? It's Meg. I must say, I was impressed with your personal note rather than a voice mail on my phone."

"You are worth that extra effort, luv."

"I would be delighted to have dinner with you this evening."

"That's marvelous, luv." He sounded genuinely thrilled by her call. "I've also procured some theater tickets for tonight. How does that sound?"

"That's terrific. Just what I need to unwind following a hard day's work." It was also just what she needed to take her mind off her disconcerting encounter with Blaine and the resurrection of feelings she thought she had purged from her life—both emotions and physical desires.

****

As Dennis finished his phone conversation with Meg, he looked up to see Blaine walking down the hallway. He rushed to the door and grabbed Blaine's attention.

"I don't know what all of these hush-hush meetings with your solicitor and banker are all about, but I saw something over the weekend I think you should know. It might have some connection. Could we step into my office to talk in private?"

Blaine looked quizzically at Dennis then followed him into the office and closed the door.

"I was out to dinner Friday night when I spotted Emily in the restaurant having dinner with a man who looked familiar, but I couldn't quite place him. On Saturday, I saw the same man in a different restaurant having dinner and what appeared to be a serious conversation with two other men, one of them being Sir Geoffrey Lewiston. Then I remembered Emily's date— Robert Templeton, Sir Geoffrey's Vice President in charge of all things underhanded, unethical, and occasionally illegal."

Blaine wrinkled his brow in concentration, then the light of realization darted across his face followed by a quick scowl of anger. He abruptly turned and hurried out of the office.

Blaine walked down the hall, pausing at Emily's desk. She had already gone for the day. He stared at the bouquet of flowers, then entered his office. Slumping into the large leather chair, he rested his elbows on the chair arms, laced his fingers together, leaned his head forward, and rested his chin against his hands. He did not move for a full fifteen minutes.

Having finally sorted things out in his mind and formulated a plan of action, he rose from his chair, turned off his light, and left the office. As he passed Dennis' office, he heard him on the phone making dinner reservations. Blaine stuck his head around the corner. "Don't you ever stay home?"

Dennis looked up and gave Blaine one of his leering

winks. "Not tonight, old boy…big date."

Blaine's manner turned serious as he walked into the office. "Listen, this business with Emily… Keep it to yourself, okay?"

"Sure, Blaine. You know me, I'm not the office gossip. Emily's social life is none of my business. I wouldn't even have mentioned it to you if it weren't for the fact that I had a real gut feeling that something was wrong. With you, your solicitor, and banker being an inseparable threesome, there's obviously something big going on. And seeing your secretary dining with the enemy…" Dennis cocked his head to one side and shot Blaine a questioning look. "I think it's safe to say that Emily is not Robert Templeton's type. Care to share what's going on?"

Blaine flashed an impish grin. "No."

"I thought not. See you tomorrow." Dennis gave Blaine a breezy wave as he headed toward the elevators.

****

After making a quick stop at his house to change clothes, Dennis drove to Meg's hotel. He couldn't stop the smile that spread across his face when she opened the door. He looked her up and down. A small whistle of appreciation escaped his lips.

She wore a red chiffon dress with a plunging neckline and back. The soft material gently caressed the swell of her breasts before winding around her slim waist and dropping in folds to just above her knees. Her high heels were a matching shade of red. She wore her hair swept up on top of her head and away from her face.

His throat went dry, his husky voice barely concealing his lustful thoughts. "Meg, my luv, you could get arrested for looking that delicious."

"Thank you. You certainly know the right things to say to make a lady feel good."

He flashed his sexiest smile as he moved closer. "I think we're going to get on famously. We shall be great friends."

She cautiously responded to his comment, her hesitation not lost on him. "Uh, yes. I, uh…I think you're probably right."

"Correct me if I'm wrong, but I have the distinct impression that there is more between you and Blaine than just having worked on an assignment together several years ago. Your reaction to seeing him in my office… Just my imagination? I certainly don't want to put myself in the way of an existing relationship."

The gamut of emotions crossing her face and the deep hurt in her eyes, left him temporarily confused. He arched one eyebrow and cocked his head. "Have I asked a wrong question? I didn't mean to make you uncomfortable."

Again, she responded with silence. He quickly recovered his charming outer manner. "I withdraw the question. It's definitely none of my business. Come, let's go to dinner." He rose to his feet and held his hand out toward her. "By the way, did I mention how marvelous you look? I shall be the envy of everyone who sees the beautiful lady on my arm." He extended his hand to assist her from the couch.

Meg again felt the charged energy of his touch. An open, easy laugh escaped her throat. She liked Dennis Mallory. She just needed to remember not to take him too seriously. Correction, rather than not taking him *too* seriously, she shouldn't take him seriously at all. "Flattery like that will go a long way with me."

"Oh? I shall certainly remember that."

A glint danced through his eyes as the heated flush rose on her cheeks. Her own words embarrassed her. She had not meant it the way he had obviously taken it. He helped her with the matching red evening wrap, then they left the suite.

As they walked down the hall, Dennis' thoughts turned to the exact nature of the relationship between Blaine and Meg. History or current? He dismissed the thoughts. If her relationship with Blaine currently existed, she would be with Blaine rather than him. That settled the matter in his mind. He classified her as fair game, and he really liked what he saw.

But that didn't stop him from harboring a slight feeling of uneasiness. Meg did not represent the type of woman he usually pursued. She had genuine class and intelligence. His choices usually gravitated toward beautiful but obviously easy women, ones who liked sex as much as he did without expecting any type of commitment. Meg did not fall into that *easy* category. His *we shall get on famously* line the others always tumbled for would not work on her. This one would definitely take more time and more charm.

Even though he could be out with any number of women who would willingly spend the night engaged in whatever games he desired, Meg was worth the extra effort. But still, he couldn't shake the nagging question about the true history between Blaine and Meg that continued to tug at the back of his mind.

Following dinner, they arrived at the theater.

"How in the world did you manage such great seats at the last minute for a popular and sold-out production? You must have some terrific connections."

"Nothing is too good for such an elegant lady." He caught the fleeting look of irritation that crossed her face at his all too obvious empty flattery. He definitely needed to proceed with more caution.

Shortly after eleven o'clock that evening, Dennis walked Meg back to her suite. He unlocked the door, snapped on the light switch, then returned her key card.

"I had a marvelous evening, Dennis. The restaurant was delightful and the play…"

He placed a kiss on her lips, sensual without being too aggressive. He felt her hesitation. "I don't know when I've enjoyed an evening more, luv. Now, I really must leave before I succumb completely to the spell you're casting over me. I'll talk to you tomorrow. Good night."

He turned away and walked down the corridor toward the elevators. His thoughts dwelled on Meg and the most effective pathway to her bed. He could not be too aggressive with her or rush her too quickly. He could tell from the tone of the evening and her slight hesitation when he kissed her that he would not get anywhere with her that night. He needed to proceed very carefully if he wanted this conquest to work.

****

As soon as Dennis left, Meg closed the door, kicked off her shoes in the living room, then went into the bedroom. After washing off all her make-up, she brushed out her hair—golden cascades falling to her shoulders.

She looked at her reflection in the mirror, not pleased with the sad expression on her face and in her eyes. She thought back to simpler times when life presented fewer complications. A moment of despair caught her as she turned away. She was about to climb into bed when she heard a knock on the door. She pulled on her robe as she started across the bedroom toward the parlor.

She spoke through the closed front door. "Who's there?"

"Meg, luv. It's Dennis. May I speak to you for a moment?"

She opened the door but did not stand aside to allow him entry to the room. "Yes, Dennis? What is it?"

"I'm so sorry for disturbing you like this but…"

Dennis slowly raked his gaze over her. His breathing quickened perceptibly. A quick jolt of apprehension darted through Meg in response to his visual intrusion.

He made eye contact with her. "I'm so sorry to be disturbing you like this. I should have phoned from the lobby. I had gotten almost to my car when I knew I had to come back to tell you again what an enchanting evening this has been and ask if you would do me the honor of dining with me again tomorrow night."

Her apprehension slowly subsided. He flashed one of his charming smiles. "I didn't want to wait until tomorrow to ask you. I wanted to be able to go to sleep knowing I would see you tomorrow night."

She relaxed and returned his smile. "Yes, I would be delighted."

"Good. I'll call for you at seven o'clock if that's acceptable."

"That will be perfect. I'm looking forward to it."

He again leaned forward and gave her a kiss, one that lingered just a little longer than the previous one. She broke it off. "Good night, Dennis."

Meg quickly closed the door as he turned to leave. An amused chuckle escaped her throat. *He uses the most absurd lines I've ever heard. I can't imagine anyone actually taking them seriously. He is fun, though, a nice diversion from the tension-filled day with Blaine.*

Yet in the back of her mind there still lingered a wariness about Dennis, so obvious about his desires, so blatant in his overtures that it was difficult to take him seriously. But could that be a mistake? In her desire to distance herself from Blaine, could she be putting herself in a bad situation with Dennis? Trading one problem for another that could end up even more troublesome? With Blaine, she knew she had no reason to be afraid of him.

Anguish rippled through her body. She slowly shook her head as the confusion welled inside her. In fact, she wasn't sure of anything anymore.

Chapter Four

Blaine had remained perched on his bar stool in the hotel's lobby bar. He watched as Dennis left the elevator and crossed the hotel lobby for the second time and exited the building. Blaine checked his watch, then headed for the elevators. He got off on Meg's floor and walked down the corridor, stopping in front of her suite. After hesitating a moment, he knocked softly at the door, then waited for an answer. Exactly what he planned to do…

A quick moment of despair shot through him. He slowly shook his head. He didn't have a clue.

The vision that greeted him when she opened the door immediately grabbed his senses and left him speechless. The natural beauty of her scrubbed face with her long hair flowing down to her shoulders, everything exactly as he remembered it from so long ago. He finally found his voice. The words came out in a spontaneous rush. "Oh, my God, Megan. You're so beautiful."

His words caught Meg completely by surprise. No one ever called her Megan, even though it was her real name. Blaine had always used it during their most intimate moments of lovemaking. Hearing his smooth, sexy voice calling her Megan sent her senses reeling. Primal urges raced through her body, settling deep inside. Her legs trembled, then turned to rubber.

Grabbing the doorjamb to steady herself, she tried

to appear casual while attempting to control her pounding heart. He stood in front of her, so close she could almost hear him breathing.

They remained perfectly still, looking into each other's eyes for a long moment. With difficulty, she managed to pull away from the control of his mesmerizing gaze. "What do you want, Blaine?" Her voice soft, her words halting. "Why are you here?"

"May I come in?"

"It's late."

"I know. I won't stay but a minute."

She hesitated, then moved aside and let him in. He closed the door, then turned to her. Placing his hands gently on her shoulders, he started to draw her to him.

She immediately shook off his touch and forced a much firmer tone to her voice than it had contained just moments ago. "Please, Blaine. Let's not have a replay of this afternoon." It took all the reserve strength she could muster to keep from melting into his embrace.

He dropped his arms to his sides, looked down at the floor, then back at her face. "You were there, so close. I couldn't stop myself."

She walked across the room, putting distance between them as she emitted an exasperated sigh before sitting on the couch. "What are you doing here?"

He cleared his throat and awkwardly shifted his weight from one foot to the other, obviously ill-at-ease. His self-conscious manner surprised her...so unlike the Blaine Reeves she had known, the confident man who knew how to handle whatever came his way.

He finally broke the silence. "I saw Dennis leave. I suspected he was your dinner date."

Her eyes narrowed as she shot him a blistering look

of disapproval. "You were *spying* on me?" Her tone carried the full force of her outrage, saying more than her words.

Blaine hadn't anticipated that reaction. He quickly shifted gears in an attempt to soothe her anger. "No, I'm not spying on you. I'm just concerned about your…about your safety."

The unexpected turn of the conversation left him uncomfortable. "Look, I'll just say what I came here to say, then I'll leave you until tomorrow. Watch yourself with Dennis. He's a terrific Managing Editor. In fact, he's the best. I'm fortunate to have him working for me, but he has the morals of an alley cat. He has a reputation from Greenwich to Hampton Court, on both sides of the Thames, as a womanizer." He searched her face for some indication of her feelings, of her reaction to his words. "I don't want you to be another of his meaningless conquests, just another notch on his bedpost."

Meg laughed. Not a becoming laugh, but one filled with sarcasm and tinged with the pain that suddenly rose to the surface. "That's rich coming from you. Which notch on your bedpost was I?" He flinched at her words, and she knew her intended sting had hit its mark. "In case you haven't noticed, I'm all grown up. I know about the hard realities of the real world. And I've had experience with men like you."

Again, her verbal darts hit their target. He had hurt her very deeply. The years of buried anger and pain had combined with the new hurt she had experienced just a few days ago when he told her about the other woman. And now all the buried emotion came out in a rush. "I can take care of myself without any interference from you, Blaine Reeves." Then the venom suddenly went out of her, leaving only the pain as her voice dropped to a mere whisper. "I've been doing it for ten years now."

He kneeled next to the couch where she sat. He lightly touched her cheek, brushed her hair back from her face, then cupped her chin in his hand as he looked deeply into her eyes. She felt him trying to delve into her thoughts, but she managed to control what she allowed him to see, not showing him any emotion at all.

"Please, Meg, be careful. To Dennis, women are just a game—play toys, something to conquer, and his usual choice of dates doesn't really require any effort for a conquest, they are very compliant—ready and very willing."

"Oh? Are you saying that I'm easy? Willing and eager to jump into bed with any man who shows me some attention?"

"Stop twisting my words."

"For your information, Dennis was a perfect gentleman the entire evening. In fact, we're going out to dinner again tomorrow night. Now, if that's all you have to say, it's late. I want to go to bed."

A sparkle appeared in his eyes as a hint of desire crossed his face. She glared at him. "Correction—I'd like to go to *sleep...alone.*"

He forced a slight smile of resignation as he stood and reached out to help her up from the couch. At first, she hesitated, then accepted his assistance. He pulled her to her feet, then drew her into his arms.

He held her to him, resting his cheek against the top of her hair. He didn't try to kiss her. He just held her, swaying slightly as they stood together in the middle of the room.

Almost as if she had no control over her own

actions, she put her arms around his waist and rested her head against his shoulder. She closed her eyes tightly as she tried to shut out her doubts, fears, and deep hurt.

He kissed the top of her hair. His words came out as a whisper. "Oh, Megan. How I've missed you."

She squeezed her eyes shut even tighter as she tried to hold back her tears. She longed for his touch, for the heated passion their lovemaking had always brought. If only the doubts and fears weren't so real and ever present.

And the intense hurt... Would the emotional pain ever go away? Would she ever heal?

He reached down, effortlessly scooped her up in his strong arms, and carried her toward the bedroom. Placing her on the bed, he leaned down to kiss her lips. She turned her face away. He gently turned her head back until she faced him as he searched questioningly for some explanation. "I would be in business meetings and suddenly realize I had no idea what was going on because my thoughts were so filled with you."

"Please don't. I can't handle this, Blaine...at least not right now."

He looked into the depths of her eyes. "We belong together. You know that as well as I do."

"I thought so, too...ten years ago. But you changed all of that when you emphatically showed me how wrong I'd been, when you abruptly walked out of my life."

He leaned over and kissed her lightly on the lips, then his kiss deepened. He probed the edges of her mouth with his tongue until she couldn't put him off any longer. Her body ached for his touch, burned with desire for his lovemaking. She opened her mouth at the same time as she ran her fingers through his thick, sandy-colored hair then circled her arms around his neck. The texture of his tongue brushed against hers. Everything so familiar, yet a decade's absence made it seem new and exciting at the same time.

His mouth staked out its claim. It demanded and took while at the same time promising and giving everything she had known in years gone by, one promise she knew he would keep.

Her breathing became labored, an excitement that matched his. Her breasts pressed against his chest, rising and falling with each breath she drew.

As he deftly untied the sash at her waist, he came in contact with her bare skin. He skimmed his hand across her shoulder, then cupped her breast in his palm eliciting a soft moan from her. He flicked the tip of his tongue across her hardened nipple several times before taking it into his mouth.

The excitement of his touch welled inside her, quickly replacing the emptiness of the last ten years. She ran her hands inside the back of his sweater, craving the feel of his bare skin. Her entire body came alive, more than at any time since he had walked out of her life and ultimately betrayed her love and trust. She tugged at his sweater, pulling it up toward his head.

Her nipple slipped from his mouth, the wet bud glistening in the soft light. He yanked off his sweater and dropped it on the floor, kicked off his shoes, then quickly did away with the rest of his clothes. He paused long enough to pull the condom packets from the pocket of his jeans and set them on the nightstand before tossing his jeans on the floor.

She looked at the packets, then shot him a quizzical look, not sure if she was irritated or amused. "You must have been pretty sure of yourself." She allowed her gaze to drift across his body, still the most perfect specimen of the male physique she had ever seen.

He shot her a sly grin. "I used to be a scout. We're always prepared." Then his expression turned serious. "Totally wishful thinking, definitely not an assumption or even a moment of confidence."

The tightness pulled across Blaine's chest as he raked his gaze across a body he had at one time intimately known so well, a body that had remained indelibly etched into his memory. She was everything any man could possibly want and all he had ever wanted. And making love only represented one small facet of that all-encompassing desire. Everything about her—the sparkle in her eyes when she laughed, her sense of humor, her intelligence, her caring and understanding, her…

He allowed the thoughts to drift away preferring not to dwell on them. One step at a time. He wanted so much more than to merely be back in her bed again. He wanted everything, wanted her to be part of his life and him part of her life—forever. The way it would have been if he hadn't behaved like a fool, hadn't done the stupidest and most reprehensible act of his life.

He wanted it all.

He eased her robe from underneath her and tossed it to the floor before stretching out next to her. He captured her mouth again with a torrid kiss. Where Dennis went for quantity, he preferred quality. He had searched for someone to share his life, someone to fill that empty place inside him. He had been involved in discreet affairs over the last ten years but none that lasted more than a few months. None that could measure up to his memory of Meg Wainwright or come close to his deep emotions that had survived the years.

He ran his hand across the swell of her breasts, down her ribcage, and along the curve of her hip. The silky smoothness of her skin stimulated his already highly aroused senses. A tremor made its way through his body attesting to the sensual impact she still had on him.

When he slipped his finger between her feminine folds, Meg sucked in a hard gasp, followed by her throaty moan of pleasure. Every heated moment of passion they had ever shared came rushing back at her. Her entire body shuddered as the exhilaration built inside her. She wanted more. Her heart pounded in her chest.

She reached for him, sensually stroking his arousal. His deep moans of excitement reached her ears, feeding her highly stimulated condition. So familiar yet so new. Enthralled by his touch, she closed her eyes and allowed the myriad sensations to flow through her body.

Blaine's chest heaved with his labored breathing. Ten years disappeared. Meg's beautiful face reflected the rapture coursing through her body, a moment he had feared he would never again be able to see, touch, or know. To never again be able to experience the unbridled joy, to share it with the only woman he had ever truly loved.

He grabbed one of the condoms, rolled it on, then nudged her legs apart. He slowly entered her, savoring every moment. Establishing a slow, smooth rhythm. Each stroke reminded him of the happiest time in his life before he had callously thrown it away in what he could only describe as a moment of temporary insanity.

Meg's ragged breathing matched his. Everything so familiar yet as exciting as a new experience. She arched her hips upward to meet each of his downward strokes. The rhythm accelerated, each moving faster, thrusting harder. Her arms and legs tightened around his body. Everything she had been craving for the last ten years convulsed in non-stop rapture.

He gave one final deep plunge and remained buried inside her. She experienced the hard spasms that shuddered through his body.

"Megan…I've missed you more than I can say…more than you'll ever realize." He smoothed back several stray tendrils of hair clinging to her damp face. He held her tightly in his embrace as he stroked her hair, pausing every few seconds to place a loving kiss on her cheek and forehead.

*****

Meg nervously awaited Blaine's arrival for the start of another location day, ready to deliver her carefully rehearsed speech the moment she saw him. They had made love two more times that night, each time more enthralling than the previous one. He had reluctantly gone home a little after three o'clock in the morning, saying he needed to get some clean clothes before that day's work and she needed to sleep.

Meg's euphoria from last night quickly turned to panic as the full impact and possible consequences of her actions seeped into her reality. No one had ever been able to propel her to the unlimited reaches of rapture the way Blaine could. No one set her soul on fire the way he did. But what had she done? What door had she opened by making love with Blaine? How would she ever be able to keep him at arm's length now?

Ten years of trying to purge him from her memory had all been destroyed in one night of heated passion. He had hurt her more than she thought possible when he had betrayed her trust and her love. She could not allow it to happen again.

As soon as he arrived for their workday, he bent over to kiss her. She quickly moved away from him. "Please, Blaine. Let's don't get anything started. Last night was a mistake. It never should have happened. This is a business relationship, nothing more, and I insist you treat it that way."

A look of shock spread across his face. "A mistake? Pretend it never happened? I couldn't do that even if I wanted to." He fixed her with a serious look. "And neither can you."

She nervously paced back and forth, purposely avoiding eye contact with him. "This is all too much, too fast." She paused for a moment as the deep hurt welled to the surface, a hurt she couldn't keep out of her voice. "You walked out on me ten very long years ago. Ten years without as much as an email from you, not even a text message. I thought I was going to die. Not a day passed that I didn't ask myself why, didn't wonder what I had done to drive you away."

She composed her emotions and continued in a stronger voice. "And now, all of a sudden, here you are with your ready explanations, assuming the last ten years will simply vanish because that's the way you want it. Or perhaps it would be more accurate to say it's the way you want it *for now*." She sucked in a steadying breath to steel her determination. "Well, it doesn't work that way. Last night was sex, nothing more. Just two consenting adults indulging a biological function. Nothing more than a one-night stand and that's all. It won't happen again. It's over. Just chalk it up to once more for old time's sake."

Having said what she had carefully prepared, she picked up her jacket and headed for the door. "Now, I have pictures to take."

He grabbed her wrist. "No you don't. Not so fast." She turned to face him, her logic and conscious determination fighting the burning desire his touch created. "Last night was a hell of a lot more than two people *indulging a biological function*. You know it as well as I do, and nothing you can say is going to change that."

"I don't know any such thing."

He slowly pulled her toward him. "I want you back in my life."

She felt her logic giving away to the mounting desires caused by the physical contact. She had to stop his tempting seduction before it passed the point of no return. "I don't want to be in your life, and I certainly don't want you in mine. This is business, remember? It's a ruse you created, nothing more than your manipulation, but still one that's strictly business."

A slight smile turned the corners of his mouth as he released her. "Okay, you win, but only for the moment." He stacked her equipment on the cart. "Let's go."

Blaine headed the car toward Regent Park and the canals of Little Venice for the start of the day's shooting. Things progressed in a very professional manner, and the work moved along efficiently. He noticed a change in her attitude. She seemed to have spent her anger and had replaced it with an indefinable sadness. And it tugged at his soul. The anger…the sadness…the hurt—all of it his fault. He vowed to do whatever it took to make things right.

If only he could figure out how to accomplish that all-important goal.

He thought they had passed the turning point last night when they made love, but he hadn't been prepared for what happened this morning. He had once again tasted paradise, then she shoved him back to square one.

They paused for a quick pub lunch. To his disappointment, she chose a table in the middle of the room rather than the intimacy of the corner booth he had indicated. She seemed to be going out of her way to reinforce what she had expressed that morning. That he could not consider lunch to be anything more than the necessity of getting something to eat. He tried to reach across the table for her hand. She quickly withdrew from his grasp while avoiding his questioning look. He had to do something, his next move driven by desperation.

"You need to shoot some night scenes for the London section. You know the type of stuff—theater patrons leaving after seeing a good play, late night dance clubs, the city lights." He kept his manner all business, belying his ulterior motives. "I have some pressing business and need to be in the office tomorrow so I think tomorrow night, after business hours, will be the best time."

She looked up at him, registering surprise at his suggestion. "Don't you have stock shots showing that type of thing."

"I suppose one of my researchers could find some, but that's not what I want. I want the style to clearly be one photographer all the way through, not some dated photos framed by someone else's creative eye." His tone and attitude left no room for disagreement.

She eyed him skeptically. "Okay…if that's your

work *orders*."

"Good. I'll pick you up at your hotel at seven o'clock tomorrow night." He glanced at his watch. "We'd better get back to work."

Blaine was very pleased with himself. The part about needing night scenes of London had some truth to it, as far as it went. More important to him, however, was making sure Meg would not be available to have dinner with Dennis. He couldn't do anything about her plans for tonight, but he could keep her too busy to see Dennis socially on future occasions until she finished the London section.

They returned to her hotel at four o'clock. He placed her equipment cart just inside the door. "I'll see you at seven tomorrow evening." He left an obviously startled Meg at the door without trying to kiss her.

Blaine hurried back to his office. He wanted to be there before Emily left for the day. He had been preoccupied most of the day by more than just the unexpected turn of events with Meg. His thoughts centered on a plan involving Emily, one he needed to put into action immediately.

He walked down the hall toward his office. He paused by Emily's desk, again noting the arrangement of flowers. Emily had a gentleman friend—a man who just happened to be Sir Geoffrey's top aide. He allowed a slight frown to wrinkle his forehead. Emily having dinner with Robert Templeton. As Dennis had said, certainly an unlikely match.

And a disturbing one.

She looked up from her work. "Mr. Reeves, is there something you require?"

"Yes, Emily. I have some changes that need to be

made to the Sinclair proposal. I'd appreciate it if you could stay a little later than normal this evening. I have an early morning breakfast meeting and will need them. Will staying late be a problem for you?"

"Of course not, Mr. Reeves. That will be no problem. All I need to do is make a quick phone call to cancel a dinner engagement for this evening."

"Perhaps you could reschedule your dinner for a little later this evening rather than cancel. We shouldn't be too late, and I'd feel bad if I caused you to miss a social engagement." He offered her a friendly smile.

She seemed very grateful for his consideration, gushing her appreciation. "Oh, thank you, Mr. Reeves. I'll just make a quick phone call, then I'm at your disposal." She reached for the phone as Blaine retreated to his office.

A few minutes later, Emily entered, a steno pad in her hand. She seated herself in the chair opposite his desk. "I'm ready, Mr. Reeves."

****

Dennis stepped forward and placed a light kiss on Meg's cheek when she greeted him at the door of her suite. He took a few moments to blatantly look her up and down. She wore a peacock blue silk dress with fitted bodice and straight skirt. "As usual, luv, you look scrumptious."

Meg smiled, graciously accepting his compliment even though she suspected it to be nothing more than a patented sequence of words he used over and over again. "Thank you, kind sir."

"Shall we go? Our reservations are waiting."

As with the previous evening, Dennis provided charming company and a lot of fun. Time passed quickly. Meg enjoyed the upbeat nature of dinner and the lively dance club where they went afterward. What a welcome change from the emotional stress of her time spent with Blaine. Her thoughts drifted for a moment. Well, not *all* the time spent with Blaine had been stressful.

She glanced at her watch—after midnight. "Will you look at the time? I was enjoying myself so much I didn't realize it was this late."

"You're not quitting on me now, are you, luv?" Dennis turned his head toward the source of the music as a rare slow song began. "One more dance. This is a nice slow one. I get to hold your body tightly against mine and whisper outrageous things in your ear."

Her spontaneous laughter said his less than subtle advances hadn't offended her. "You don't need to whisper in my ear to convince me you're outrageous. I'm already convinced."

Following the last dance, he escorted her back to her hotel suite. The hour had grown late, and she was tired. Instead of inviting him in, she turned at the door and blocked his way. "I had a marvelous evening, Dennis. Good food, charming company, and a fun time dancing."

His manner turned serious, in contrast to her ebullience. "It was my pleasure, luv. Thank you for sharing another delightful evening with me." He lowered his head to hers and captured her mouth with a kiss that quickly escalated.

Meg allowed the kiss to continue until the moment he slipped his tongue between her lips. She quickly pulled away from him, breaking the contact. "I think…I think we'd best call it an evening. Goodnight, Dennis."

She quickly went inside, closing the door behind

her.

She took a moment to compose herself before continuing on to the bedroom. She reflected on his aggressive kiss and recalled Blaine's words of warning. This thing with Dennis had suddenly taken a sharp turn.

An enjoyable evening, a carefree time with an interesting dinner companion. That's all she wanted—nothing more. She was glad to have had a legitimate excuse to turn down his dinner invitation for the next evening, relieved to be able to say she would be working. She had, however, promised to have dinner with him the following night.

Perhaps she had been too hasty in saying yes.

****

Robert walked Emily to her front door after their fifth date—their fifth *real* date, more than just having tea together. She lived her entire life, all forty-nine years of it, with her parents in a modest house in a blue-collar working-class neighborhood. Robert was the first gentleman caller to walk her to her front door. In fact, her first gentleman caller ever.

When they reached her front door, Robert took her house key from her hand and inserted it into the lock. Before unlocking the door, he turned to her. "Emily, I hope you don't think me presumptuous, especially after such a short acquaintanceship, but I would very much like to kiss you and would be honored if you would allow it."

"Oh, Robert…" Her voice soft, his attentions leaving her overwhelmed. "You just embarrass me so. "I've never—"

He placed his fingertips beneath her chin and lifted, then leaned his face forward and cut off her words by pressing his lips against hers. As kisses go, a very chaste kiss. After a moment, he pulled back. "I hope I wasn't being too forward. I wouldn't want to do anything that would make you feel your principles had been compromised."

Emily's legs felt weak, and her heart pounded. She had never before had an attractive man treat her as if she were someone special, take her to such nice places, and now, he had actually kissed her, the sensations almost too much for her to handle. In another two months, she would be fifty years old. She had given up on ever finding a nice gentleman to share her life…until now.

"Oh, Robert. That was the most exciting thing I've ever experienced."

He smiled, his practiced charm covering her like a warm blanket. "I'm so glad you weren't offended. I'll call you tomorrow." He unlocked the door and handed her the key.

She entered the house and closed the door. Her thoughts wandered back to their initial accidental meeting. It had been a Saturday. As she did each Saturday, she had spent the afternoon at the library. With several books clasped in her hands, she'd hurried to the underground station to catch the train home. As she descended the stairs into the station, Robert suddenly appeared from around the corner and bumped into her, knocking her books to the ground.

Her mind still had trouble accepting her good fortune. This distinguished, attractive man had picked up her books, made sure he hadn't hurt her, then engaged her in conversation. Before she knew what was happening, she found herself in a restaurant seated across the table from him enjoying a cup of tea. Her senses had been in a delirious whirl of happiness ever since. At the age of forty-nine she had found a gentleman caller.

Her life had taken on an entirely new meaning.

Chapter Five

Blaine arrived at his office at seven the next morning. He had spent two days away from a hectic schedule in order to be with Meg, and now, he had the added pressure of the problems with the Sinclair package. His first order of business was a phone call to Harry to fill him in on what had transpired. He suspected it would be a couple of days before there would be any viable feedback from his little charade.

As he settled into his chair, he grabbed a file folder from the corner of his desk. He opened the file, stared at the contents, then shoved it aside. Leaning back in his chair with his eyes closed, he thought back to simpler times when he had been art director at the magazine in Los Angeles. When he and Meg had been together, happy, and in love.

He sat up straight and looked around his plush office. He had come a long way from those days in Los Angeles. Luck had favored him. All his hard work had paid off, but it didn't mean a thing without being able to share it with Meg.

He returned his attention to the papers on his desk and forced his concentration to the work at hand. Another hour and the hallways and offices began to fill with the work activities of the day.

"Good morning, Mr. Reeves." Emily entered his office carrying a cup of coffee, which she placed on his desk.

"Good morning, Emily. I didn't expect you in this early. I told you to come in late to make up for the time I kept you last night. I appreciate you staying to make those changes." He carefully chose his words, not wanting to create any suspicion in her mind.

"That was most kind of you. I appreciate the offer, but there is work to be done."

Her entire manner seemed to radiate a glow of contentment. She actually looked happy, a disposition he had never associated with her before. He picked up the coffee cup and took a sip as he watched her return to the outer office. Now it was just a matter of time. He would soon know if his false information had been passed on and if so, to whom. He did not like the waiting, the feeling of not having control over a situation that belonged to him, something he had initiated. It made him anxious.

Blaine left his office and headed down the hall just as Dennis entered from the stairs. He noted Dennis' bouncy step and whistling as he walked toward his office. The whistling in particular caught Blaine's attention, something Dennis did when particularly pleased about the outcome of some deal—both business and personal.

A quick jab of anger hit Blaine as he wondered if Dennis' good mood reflected his dinner date with Meg last night. He took a calming breath, trying not to show any irritation. "You seem in a pretty upbeat mood this morning."

Dennis acknowledged Blaine's presence with a big grin. "I've got a manuscript on my desk that's going to knock your socks off. An unknown author, never before published, and we have first crack at him. I'm telling you, we've got a best seller on our hands…an international best seller." A thoughtful look crossed his face. "Of course, we might have to translate it from British into American before we can release it in the States."

Blaine shook his head as he tried to suppress a grin. It was Dennis' favorite jab at him, teasing him about the differences in the two branches of the English language. Blaine returned his jesting manner, relieved that Dennis' good mood apparently had nothing to do with Meg. "If you order up that expense, it'll come out of your paycheck."

"That's cold, Mr. Reeves. Here I am knocking myself out for you and this is how you treat me." He gave Blaine a quick wink, then turned toward his office. His voice trailed off as he walked down the hall. "Yes indeed, Mr. Reeves…very cold."

****

The look on Sir Geoffrey's face clearly defined his mood, the news Robert had brought him not at all what he expected. His voice carried the full force of his anger. "What the hell is the meaning of this? Everything was established leaving only the matter of price. Now, all of a sudden, the entire negotiation is back at the beginning with all these new contingencies." His beady eyes narrowed to a mere slit as he glared at Robert. "Are you sure of your information? Is it possible this secretary is on to your real intentions?"

Robert shifted uncomfortably in his chair. "She doesn't suspect a thing."

Sir Geoffrey relaxed a bit, leaning back in his chair. "Very well." His lips pursed into a hard, thin line. He waved his hand, dismissing Robert's presence.

Robert quickly left the office. He thoroughly disliked these intense interrogations Sir Geoffrey periodically subjected him to almost as much as he disliked some of the things he was required to do, things such as dating Emily in order to procure information from her.

At first it didn't matter. It was all part of the job. He knew he had very few scruples left. He had sold his ethics and integrity to Sir Geoffrey in exchange for a huge paycheck. But when he realized just how naïve and vulnerable Emily was, he felt definite pangs of guilt.

His personal feelings would not change things, though. He would continue to provide whatever services Sir Geoffrey required no matter how distasteful and continue to bank his huge paycheck along with the bonuses for the particularly unpleasant tasks—such as this one.

****

Meg opened the door of her suite that evening and admitted Blaine. He reached for her, but she deftly avoided him. "It's business, Blaine. It's just business and nothing more. How many times do I need to say that?"

"How about as many times as it's going to take for me to believe you really mean it. So far, you're not even close."

She averted her gaze, avoiding what she knew to be his questioning look. Being upset didn't excuse her for snapping at him a little too quickly. It had been a day of reflection with neither Blaine nor Dennis around to cloud her thinking. And now, she felt even more confused than she had been when all of this started.

Dennis offered a lot of fun. Terribly obvious but fun.

Blaine, on the other hand, had been the one great love of her life who had hurt her more than she thought possible. Now, he suddenly appeared on the scene, wanting to pick up where they left off as if nothing had happened.

She should have refused to take the assignment and left as soon as she found out Blaine owned Pendragon. He probably wouldn't have actually sued her over breach of contract. But now, it was too late, too late for her to refuse the assignment. She couldn't turn back the clock. She had started work and needed to finish, the sooner the better.

And to make things worse, she had compromised what she kept insisting was strictly business by spending a night in bed with him. True, it had been an incredible night of making love that left her totally satiated yet still wanting more. But it had been a horrible mistake, one she didn't dare repeat.

"Have you already eaten?" Blaine interrupted her thoughts. "I hope not because I haven't, and I'm hungry."

"Well, I had a late lunch."

He shot her one of his dazzling smiles, causing his dimples to show as he reached for her equipment laden photo cart. "Good. Our first stop will be dinner."

"Blaine—"

He held up his right hand as if swearing an oath. "Business, Meg." His expression conveyed all seriousness. "Strictly business."

Dinner went smoother than she expected. She insisted on eating in a crowded pub rather than the quiet, out of the way restaurant Blaine had chosen. She carefully kept the conversation to impersonal topics, safe things that would not cause her emotions to run wild.

However, she could not control the underlying layer of sensual desire that continued to course through her veins. An unnerving awareness that told her how much she wanted him back in her bed. And back in her life.

Following dinner, they spent the rest of the evening shooting various aspects of London night life. They didn't get back to her hotel until a little after one in the morning. They rode up in the elevator in silence, each absorbed in personal thoughts.

He took her key card from her hand, unlocked the door to the suite, then returned the card to her. After stepping aside so she could enter the room, he started to follow her. She quickly turned toward him, blocking his way. Her tentative words and hesitation conveyed the emotional tension shoving at her reality. "It's pretty late, and eight o'clock in the morning will be here too soon."

His soft reply reflected his fatigued condition. "Why don't we start at ten tomorrow morning rather than eight? Is that okay with you?"

"Yes, that would be much better." Relief settled over her. She held his gaze for a long moment. The emotion she saw in the depths of his eyes made her very uncomfortable. She felt herself being drawn in, betrayed by her own undeniable feelings and desires. She nervously played with the gold chain that adorned her neck as she cleared her throat in an attempt to shake the tightness. "Well…as I said, it's late. Goodnight, Blaine."

He wheeled her equipment cart across the threshold into her suite, brushed his fingertips lightly across her cheek, then leaned forward to kiss her. His intoxicating nearness chipped away at her resolve. A shiver darted through her body forcing her to take a step backward out of his reach.

She tried to make her voice as stern as possible. "Goodnight."

Meg quickly shut the door, closing out the unnerving effect he still had on her, a situation not helped by her earlier weakness in giving in to her desires for the one man she could not resist no matter how much she tried. The one man she couldn't stop loving.

She undressed, climbed into bed, and closed her eyes. She desperately wanted to fall asleep immediately, to avoid the thoughts that circulated through her mind. Thoughts about Blaine and the passion he stirred in her, thoughts about the intensity of the lovemaking they had shared so many years ago.

And the lovemaking they shared again just a night ago.

She had to be strong, to ignore the desires coursing through her veins. She finally fell asleep, but the thoughts and desires did not go away. They continued to haunt her dreams.

****

After leaving Meg's hotel, Blaine drove straight home, a newly restored brick building on the south bank of the Thames with a view of Tower Bridge and the Tower of London across the river. The flat had large expanses of glass interspersed with decorative wood paneling. It included a master bedroom suite, two guest bedrooms each with private bath, an office, kitchen with eating area, and a formal dining room. He had separated the large living room into areas by furniture groupings including a wet bar and informal seating arrangement in a corner. There was also a guest bathroom located between the living room and dining room.

Large windows overlooked the Thames River,

skylights let in additional brightness. There were two fireplaces, one in the master bedroom suite and one in the living room with another seating area—the look and feel of the decor similar to Pendragon's offices, both representative of Blaine Reeves' artistic hand, keen eye, and elegant taste.

The most unusual thing found in Blaine's surroundings was a collection of books, magazines, posters, pictures, invitations, and newspaper clippings. The collection represented every article and photograph by Meg published in magazines, the two books that included collections of her photographs, invitations to gallery showings, and reviews of her work—the collection one hundred percent complete. He had hired a service in the States to scour all media for any word of her work and to forward them to him. Two of Meg's original photographs hung on his living room wall. Both photographs had been purchased anonymously, one from a gallery in San Francisco and the other from a showing in New York.

Blaine pulled his easel from the storage closet and set it up in the living room, then he unwrapped a new canvas. It had been a long time since he had actually taken charcoal in hand to begin sketching on canvas, the way he always started an oil painting. He worked quickly, like someone obsessed with an image that must be captured before it faded from memory. His entire demeanor seemed transformed as he worked on the sketch. The intense set of his jaw relaxed. The exhaustion he had experienced earlier seemed to disappear as the image took shape.

****

At precisely ten o'clock the next morning, Meg

opened the door to greet Blaine. He bent to kiss her, but she avoided him by saying they needed to get to work. She had spent a miserable night tossing and turning in her sleep, what little sleep she could claim. The situation had become so complicated. She had become so confused.

They immediately went to work, Meg thankful for the professional attitude that surrounded the day as they proceeded through the work schedule.

Blaine thought about Meg's dinner date with Dennis for that night. He picked up on her confusion and knew how vulnerable she would be to Dennis' advances. He also accepted full responsibility for creating her emotional state, but that didn't make his fears any less valid. He had watched Dennis work his charms on unsuspecting women and knew just how persuasive the man could be.

How could he protect Meg from Dennis without appearing to be spying on her? He saw her as precariously balanced on a tightrope. If he didn't proceed cautiously, he would be responsible for her falling off, and Dennis would be the net that caught her.

When she left for the countryside, he wouldn't be able to go with her. He still had a publishing house to run, and right now, that included what had turned out to be very tricky negotiations complicated by meddling from a competitor. He simply could not be out of town.

Then a sudden realization struck him, shocking him out of his thoughts. It did sound as if he was spying on her. Exactly where did that line lie between spying and protecting? He sucked in a steadying breath as he slowly shook his head. He held that breath for a long moment before exhaling. He would have to struggle with his conscience and that particular dilemma at some other time. Right now, he needed to guard her safety, a safety he had inadvertently put in jeopardy.

They finished the day of location shooting and arrived back at her suite about four o'clock. Blaine deposited her photo cart by the door, then headed toward the bar.

Meg looked at her watch. "Dennis is picking me up at seven o'clock, but I suppose there's time for you to have a *quick* drink before you go."

He poured each of them a glass of wine. As she took the glass from him, their fingers brushed lightly. She jerked her hand away just as he let go of the glass. It tumbled to the floor and bounced on the carpeting spilling the contents. They each grabbed a towel from the bar and converged on the wet carpeting to mop up the wine. While on the floor, their hands touched again.

Meg froze in place, afraid to look at him. She knew if she met his gaze, if she could see the emotion in his eyes, she would be lost to her own desires. Desires both physical and emotional. She knew those desires would betray the logic of what she had to do. Her intention had been to keep her distance from his mesmerizing pull. Did she have the resolve to carry through with her plan? At that moment she wasn't sure of anything, certainly not her ability to maintain her distance from the enticing Blaine Reeves.

Blaine quickly moved to her side and lifted her chin so he could look into her eyes. Again, he saw the confusion and hurt. He put his arms around her and drew her close. He felt her initial resistance, but it slowly faded as he continued to hold her. He cradled her head against his shoulder, stroking her hair as he rocked her in his arms.

"Oh, Megan. What kind of insanity took hold of me ten years ago?" His words came out as a sigh as much as spoken. "How could I have done this to you?"

Her body trembled as tears slid silently down her cheeks, wetting his shirt. He raised her chin and looked into her tear-filled eyes. He bent his head and tenderly kissed each eyelid, tasting the saltiness. "I wish I could give you a thousand kisses for every tear I've caused you. Tell me, Megan, what can I do? How do I win back your trust and have you as part of my life again?"

She took a steadying breath. "I don't know, Blaine. I don't know." Her words were barely audible. "Perhaps it's too late."

He tightened his arms around her and tried to ward off the fear that shuddered inside him. "Don't say that. It's not too late." His voice turned into a whisper, a frightened whisper. "I won't allow it to be too late."

She gave him a weak smile as he gently brushed the tears from her cheeks. "This is a fine mess we have here, isn't it?"

He glanced at his watch, then tentatively broached what he knew would be a tricky subject as he continued to rock her in his arms. "I'd like you to cancel your dinner date with Dennis."

Meg jerked her head back as her anger flared. "So that's what this is all about. Nothing more than empty words. An attempt to lull me into doing what you want." She angrily jumped to her feet. "How dare you think you can come strolling back into my life after ten long years and tell me what to do. I find Dennis charming and his company enjoyable. I don't need you. I'm perfectly capable of taking care of myself."

She stormed to the door of the suite and yanked it open. "Now, please leave. I have to get ready for my *date*." She glared defiantly at him, tears streaming down her cheeks. When he made no effort to move, she repeated her demand with more emphasis. "I want you to leave right now!"

He reluctantly walked to the door. He reached out to touch her cheek. She quickly shoved his hand away.

"Megan—"

"Get out!"

Sorrow and despair churned inside Blaine as he walked slowly down the corridor toward the elevators. Thousands of emotions and thoughts collided inside him. How could he have handled that so stupidly? In trying to protect her delicate vulnerability from Dennis' clutches, he had ended up driving her away from him and toward the very person who represented the danger. Dennis was like a shark that smelled blood. He would sense her vulnerability and move in for the conquest—surely and swiftly.

Blaine clenched his fists and set his jaw in a hard line. How could he stop this without driving Meg away from him forever? Or a more frightening thought. After working hard to manipulate circumstances so he could win her back, had he already driven her away for the final time? He took the elevator to the lobby and went home.

He tossed his jacket across the back of a chair and went directly to the bar where he fixed himself a stiff drink. He took a sip of his scotch as he slumped onto the couch and watched the river traffic on the Thames. They had made love with an intensity that scorched the very depth of his soul. He knew, he felt it with every fiber of his being, she had been on the brink of forgiving him and allowing him back into her life—not just into her bed. Allowing that they had a future together, something tangible and real.

Then he stupidly blew it. In thirty seconds, he lost every bit of ground he had gained. This was worse than being back at square one. He no longer battled her hurt from ten years ago plus the obvious shock he had handed her when he had tried to explain what had really happened. Just an hour ago, he had added a whole new level to her mistrust and anger.

He slowly sipped his scotch—too many things up in the air, too many problems pulling his emotional strings. He knew he had neglected his business because of his all-consuming need to concentrate on Meg.

Too many complications. Too little time.

A sudden thought brightened his dismal mood. He sat up straight. The answer to his immediate problem with Meg? His sister. He would buy Crista a plane ticket and have her come for a visit. Neither of her sons were living at home anymore.

The last time he had talked to her, she was in the process of divorcing Jack. She would probably welcome the change of scenery. He checked his watch to determine the time in New York, then reached for the phone and dialed his sister's number.

"Crista, it's Blaine. What would you say to dropping everything and coming to London for a month? I can use your help with something."

"What's the matter?" Her voice contained a hint of alarm. "Are you in some kind of trouble?"

"No…not really…" He paused mid-sentence leaving dead air on the phone line.

"Blaine? Are you still there?"

"Uh…yeah."

"What's wrong?"

He heard the deep concern in Crista's voice. "It's Meg."

"Meg?" Crista's genuine shock raced along the phone connection.

"Yes. She's here. I hired her to photograph and write a new travel book, and, uh, well…" The proper words to explain his plight refused to materialize, words that wouldn't make it sound as manipulative as the reality of the situation.

"*And, uh*? You're more articulate than that. What kind of a sentence is *and, uh*? Let me guess. You thought you'd get her to London—she probably didn't even know it was your company—and the moment she saw you she would magically fall into your arms and forgive you for everything that happened. Things would be just the way they were ten years ago before you screwed it up big time. You assumed you could take up right where you left off and live happily ever after. Am I close?"

A combination of irritation and embarrassment forced the words out of his mouth. "Dammit, Crista. It's bad enough that you can usually read me like a book. At least let me tell it my own way." A sigh of resignation escaped his throat. "You are, of course, right."

"So, what's your problem?"

"Well, first of all she hasn't been in a forgiving mood. Second, there's Dennis Mallory."

"What's Dennis have to do with this?"

"You know Dennis. He tries to get every woman who crosses his path into his bed. He has taken Meg out to dinner a couple of times, and they're going out again tonight. He has his sights set on her."

"And just what do you think I can do about that?"

"I want you to keep an eye on Meg. See that Dennis doesn't take advantage of her. Right now, she's in a very vulnerable state, and I, uh, might even have to accept a little bit of responsibility for that." He cleared his throat. "Just a little while ago I asked her to cancel her date with Dennis for tonight."

"And?"

"Let's just say she didn't take kindly to my suggestion." Blaine took a steadying breath in an attempt to calm his rising panic. "That's why I need you here, Crista. Help me make sure Dennis doesn't seduce her, that she'll be safe. I can't let her become just another of his nameless conquests."

Crista chuckled. "Nameless conquests. That's Dennis all right. Have you ever wondered why he calls every woman *luv*? It's so he won't get them confused and accidentally call one by someone else's name."

"Come on, Crista. What do you say? Will you come? Right away? Like tonight?"

"This whole thing, tricking Meg into being there…" Crista's tone conveyed her thoughts as clearly as her words. "This is, without a doubt, the dumbest thing you have ever done with the single exception of when you walked out on her originally."

"Okay, it's dumb. But will you do it? I'll have a pre-paid ticket for you at the airline counter for whatever flight you want."

"Your idea is dumb, but your timing is perfect. The court date for my divorce was last week. I'm now a free woman. The last several months have been really rough. I can definitely use the change of scenery. Manhattan is beginning to close in around me. I'll be glad to come for a visit, but…" She put extra emphasis on her next words. "I *won't* be your spy."

That word *spy* again. He dismissed it as something to wrestle with at another time. Crista had agreed to come to London, and that was what mattered. "That's great."

"That ticket will be first class, won't it?" she teased.

"Oh? You wanted to fly first class? I've heard coach is very comfortable. Or maybe we can compromise. How about business class?" They talked a few more minutes, then he concluded the conversation.

Blaine smiled. Everything would work out. Crista would help him with his Dennis problem. He'd talk her into it when he could sit down with her in person.

In the interim, he needed to postpone Meg's departure for the countryside until after Crista arrived. He would tell her she had to identify each of the London pictures and write a rough draft of that section before she started on the rest of the book. He would see to it that she didn't have any time to spend with Dennis over the weekend. She would be working with Dennis in the offices for a couple of days, but one thing he could say for Dennis… He was conscientious about his work and would not make a move on her there.

Blaine leaned back, pleased with himself. Very pleased, indeed.

****

Dennis busied himself preparing for his dinner date with Meg, his attitude upbeat. If he played his cards right, he would be able to talk her into having dinner in her suite where they would only be a few steps from her bedroom.

A quick twinge of doubt stabbed at him. He

immediately shook it off. He had neither the time nor the desire to be concerned with doubts. He continued to look in the mirror as he put a perfect Windsor knot in his monogrammed silk tie.

Meg would certainly be the cream of the crop, the top notch on his bedpost, an expression Blaine had used after listening to him tell about his latest sexual exploits. Blaine was one of those *one woman man* types. Not nearly as much fun as he could be.

This would be a night to remember, one for the scrapbook. Again, he felt a sharp emotional stab. Could it possibly be a guilty conscience? Nagging thoughts about the exact nature of the relationship between Meg and Blaine continued to push at the back of his mind.

He had to admit that of late he had been doing a bit, albeit a very small bit, of soul searching concerning his lifestyle. Lord knew he'd slept with enough women, all of them beautiful and some of them even able to carry on a simple conversation as long as there weren't too many multi-syllable words or a topic that required more knowledge than glancing at headlines on social media. But real friends? He didn't have anyone he could simply hang out with, to use one of those American expressions he had become so fond of lately. He didn't have any male friends where they were just *the guys,* and he certainly didn't have any platonic female friends. Well, except maybe one.

That one, surprisingly, was Blaine's sister. He had met Crista eight years ago on what turned out to be one of her many visits to see Blaine. At first, he tried to hit on her out of habit even though she was Blaine's sister, but she set him straight real quick. He would never forget her exact words.

You know, Dennis, if I weren't married I'd sure give some real serious consideration to your numerous and outrageous propositions. But I am married so that's the end of this discussion.

Even though he made it a point to never date married or engaged women, he had been willing to make an exception for Crista. He appreciated her intelligence and wit, had always liked her honest, forthright manner. No cute little games, no talking in circles, no coy gestures or mannerisms. Just straightforward statements.

Actually, as he reflected, he had to admit it was refreshing to spend an innocent evening with a woman. He still talked about ravishing her body, but they both knew he said it jokingly, and that's as far as it would go. He would never do anything to compromise or hurt her. Or to damage their genuine friendship.

But for the most part, the women he knew were at their best when horizontal. He allowed a little chuckle. He and Blaine had engaged in many discussions over that one with Blaine accusing him of not having any respect for women. It wasn't true, of course. He had a great deal of respect for Crista...and Meg. And for that matter, most women. His dates, however, were another story. He usually chose his dates based on hot sex rather than any attempt to build a relationship or even be just friends, women who were looking for the same thing as him.

He again looked at himself in the mirror. He and Blaine... Blaine Reeves represented the closest thing he had to a real friend, and he wasn't sure Blaine actually liked him as a person.

He shook his head to rid himself of the troublesome thoughts. At the age of forty-four, was he actually experiencing some sort of regret at his lifestyle? Some semblance of a guilty conscience? No way. Tonight, he was looking forward to a very special treat. A nice dinner and Meg for dessert.

Chapter Six

As soon as Meg opened the door of the suite, Dennis immediately sensed something wrong. She looked beautiful, but he saw a distant sadness in her eyes and a somewhat distraught demeanor in spite of her dazzling smile and warm, gracious outer manner. He found himself experiencing a very foreign emotion—concern for her and a desire to comfort and care for her rather than use her emotional vulnerability to take advantage of her.

That annoying twinge stabbed at him again. He mentally shook it off. He didn't have time or the desire to deal with some errant pangs of guilt. A very desirable woman in an obviously emotional and upset state, something that could surely be turned to his advantage. Then the thought popped into his mind. Maybe Blaine had been right. Maybe he really was nothing more than an unprincipled bastard. At the time Blaine had said it, he had used a joking tone of voice and the two of them had not been engaged in any type of argument, but the words stuck in his mind.

He shook away the unwanted feelings and immediately assumed the manner of a very concerned friend. "Meg, luv, what's wrong? Are you okay? Here. Come sit down."

Dennis took her hand and led her to the couch. He sat close to her. "Is there anything I can do?"

He put his arm around her shoulder and pulled her to him in a comforting manner, talking softly and tenderly. She offered some initial resistance to his subtle aggression, but then she seemed to give up all pretense at bravery and surrendered to his soothing manner.

He pulled her into his arms and gently kissed her cheek. "What can I do, luv? It's so painful for me to see you like this. What happened? Where is that enchanting carefree spirit I've come to know and care about?"

She started to pull away from his arms. "I'm sorry, Dennis. I must apologize for my—"

He immediately put his fingers to her lips. "Now, luv. You don't owe me any apologies or explanations, unless it would make you feel better to talk about it." He continued to talk to her in a gentle voice, the epitome of the caring concerned friend. "We've only known each other for a few days, but during that time I've grown fond of you...very fond. I want to help you forget whatever it is that has you so upset."

He placed his fingers under her chin and tilted her face up so he could look into her eyes to gauge the effects of his words. An incredible vulnerability mixed with her confusion. The slightest hint of a smile tugged at his lips, a smile he immediately covered by burying his face in her hair and tenderly kissing the top of her head. He loosened his necktie and unfastened the top button of his shirt as he congratulated himself. Tonight would definitely be the night. He finished removing the necktie and hurriedly tried to stuff it in his suit coat pocket but missed the mark with the tie, dropping it to the floor instead. He started to reach for it, then she shifted her weight in his arms, drawing his attention back to her.

Meg experienced a multitude of conflicting

emotions. She became vaguely aware of Dennis becoming more sensually aggressive as he talked to her and held her in his arms. Blaine's warning briefly danced through her mind again, but she immediately dismissed it. She had been emotionally alone for so long. Blaine had been the measure against which every man for the last ten years had been judged. All had emerged lacking. No one had been able to compete with her memory of Blaine. And then the torrid lovemaking they had shared two nights ago—a definite mistake, but a reality she couldn't deny.

Dennis stunned her out of her thoughts when he captured her mouth with his, pulling her tightly against his body. He kissed her with a fire that conveyed pure lust, his hot tongue attacking with a surprising aggressiveness. He consumed her with the swiftness of an out-of-control wildfire.

A surge of panic grabbed Meg. She pulled back and looked into his eyes. The soft sensuality and caring emotion had disappeared. She saw only a primal sex drive. She held his gaze for a brief moment, then the realization of the message she had unintentionally conveyed to him fully hit her.

She tried to push him away. "I…this isn't—"

He quickly recaptured her mouth. He kissed her roughly, forcing his tongue between her lips.

Her mind reeled as she tried to shove away from his aggression. No matter how much she wanted to drive Blaine from her thoughts and desires, she didn't want to do it this way. She struggled in Dennis' embrace, fighting against his tight hold on her. The gentle caring man who had been with her just a few minutes earlier had disappeared to be replaced by this stranger.

Panic jolted through her followed by genuine fear. Her heart pounded. She tried to pull her head away from him while pushing harder against his chest with her hands. Instinctively, she slapped his face.

The sound of the slap shocked Dennis more than the sting of her hand. He turned loose of her and jerked back. "What the hell—"

Then he saw the look of terror on her face and the fear in her eyes. His momentary pique instantly changed to shock, then alarm. What just happened truly rattled him more than anything in his entire life, leaving him shaken and unnerved.

"My God. Meg…I'm so sorry. I didn't mean—"

The look of terror slowly faded from her face, but the fear lingered in the depths of her eyes. Dennis reached his hand out to her. She immediately scooted away from him.

"Meg…please. I just wanted you so badly. I…I didn't mean to…" He didn't know what to say. A lump formed in his throat, and his mouth went dry. Anxiety churned in the pit of his stomach. For the first time in his life, his glib manner, ready charm, and easy words totally deserted him leaving distress, anguish, and deep shame in its wake.

She seemed to regain some of her composure. "I think it's best if this incident—if this entire evening— was forgotten as if it never happened." Her voice took on more authority. "I want you to leave—now."

He again reached his hand toward her. She rose from the sofa and took a couple of steps away. He dejectedly dropped his hand to his side and stared at the floor.

He looked up at her again. "I'm so very sorry, luv. I really am. I promise you it won't ever happen again.

When I saw that look of terror on your face and the fear in your eyes, I… It really scared me. I'm sorry, Meg. Please believe me. I've never done anything like that before. I'm so very sorry…and so ashamed. I'll go now."

He left the suite without looking back. He had never been confused where women were concerned. Everything had always been so clear and definitive, until now. He had just attempted to force himself on a very special woman to the point where he actually frightened her. His actions were those of some low-life creature. He had never before tried to force himself on a woman. The anxiety churning in his stomach turned to a sick feeling, one that twisted his insides into tight knots telling him just how totally disgusting and reprehensible his actions had been.

He walked out of the hotel and checked his watch—only eight-thirty. He desperately needed something to soothe his conscience and settle the deep guilt rampaging unchecked through his consciousness. He would hit some of his usual haunts and find a willing playmate to take his mind off of tonight, to help him wipe away what had happened. But deep inside, he knew that was impossible. He would never forget what had happened. It was a disgrace of the worst kind that would continue to live in his memory and haunt his life.

He glanced back inside the hotel lobby. What must Meg be thinking right now?

He shook his head. Probably better he didn't know.

****

Meg emerged from the bedroom at eight o'clock the next morning in response to the knock on her door. It had been three o'clock that morning before she finally drifted off into a fitful sleep and as a result had overslept. She opened the door and motioned Blaine inside. "I'll be ready in just a minute. Have a seat."

She went back into the bedroom, leaving him in the living room. She closed the bedroom door, making it clear he was not welcome to follow her.

As he aimlessly wandered around while waiting on her, his gaze lit on a necktie on the floor by the sofa. He picked it up and immediately spotted Dennis' monogram. A hard jab of anger flashed through him as he quickly shoved the tie into his jacket pocket. He looked toward her bedroom.

An uncontrollable pang of despair shoved at him, followed by a rush of intense anger as he thought about Dennis making love to her. His emotions ran wild. He wasn't sure where to direct his anger, to Dennis or to Meg.

His thoughts stopped. Angry with Meg? He could never be angry with her, especially for something he knew to ultimately be his fault.

She emerged from the bedroom, ready for the day's shooting. "Sorry to keep you waiting."

Blaine tried to sound casual. "How was your dinner with Dennis last night?"

He noted the quick look that darted across her face, then disappeared, one he instantly interpreted as guilt.

She avoided eye contact with him. "Oh, we ended up not going to dinner."

Again, his anger flared as he set his jaw in a hard line. Dennis had gone too far this time, taking advantage of her vulnerability. A hard lump settled in the pit of Blaine's stomach. A vulnerability for which he knew he had to take total responsibility. He grabbed the equipment cart and went out the door, leaving a surprised

Meg standing in the middle of the room.

Among the locations for the day were Hyde Park, St. James Park, and Green Park. Meg wanted to capture the peaceful setting of the parks and contrast it with the hustle and bustle of the shopping areas. The day's shooting proceeded on schedule and without incident, but the undercurrent of tension refused to go away. Blaine seemed to be rushing her, as if he wanted the day to be over as quickly as possible.

At three o'clock, Meg shot her last pictures at the final location for the day. "Well, that does it for London. I'll be starting on the countryside in the morning."

Blaine's manner turned elusive and vague. "I want you to spend Monday and Tuesday at the offices. Your London pictures need to be individually identified and a rough draft for that section of the book must be completed before you leave. We have a very tight schedule on this book. It needs to be completed in segments. You can start the countryside as soon as you finish the London section."

A sense of foreboding settled over her. That was not at all what she wanted to hear. "Very well. I'll be at the office at nine o'clock Monday morning."

He cocked his head to one side and shot her a questioning look. "You seem less than pleased. Do you have a problem with that?"

"No. Of course not."

"Good. I'll send the limo for you."

"There's no need. I can take a taxi."

When he dropped her at the hotel, he seemed in a hurry to leave. He didn't even try to kiss her. Something was very wrong. Her sense of guilt over the possibility of having unintentionally misled Dennis told her Blaine somehow knew what had happened, knew about her momentary weakness with Dennis. Even though her actions were none of Blaine's business, that didn't ease her guilt.

Blaine stormed out of the hotel and headed straight back to the Pendragon offices. He had business to take care of, business concerning the information leak about the Sinclair deal. But first, he had something more important to deal with. He marched directly to Dennis' office, burst through the door, and slammed it shut behind him. He threw the necktie on the desk. "Do you want to take a wild guess where I found this?"

Dennis' startled expression faded as he picked up the tie. "I was wondering what happened to that."

Blaine lunged across the desk and grabbed the front of Dennis' shirt in his fist. An intense anger surged through his body. "Don't you ever touch her again."

"Touch who?" Then the realization flashed in his eyes, the one saying he just remembered dropping the tie in Meg's suite.

"You know damn well who I'm talking about."

Dennis angrily jumped to his feet, pulling Blaine's hands away. "Oh? And just when did she become your property?"

Blaine's eyes flashed angry blue fire. "The lady isn't *property*."

Dennis' attitude turned just as volatile, his voice just as hard. "You say she's not property? Then stop acting like you own her. Stop behaving like an ass."

The two men glared at each other. Dennis saw the pain mixed with anger that covered Blaine's face. His manner softened a little. "I don't know the history between you two, but I do know Meg's hurting really badly, and it's because of you, something you did."

"And you thought it was your civic duty to help take her mind off of it, right?" The two men continued to glare at each other as Blaine's anger visibly started to drain away. "It's something that happened a long time ago. Something I'm not proud of."

"Blaine, don't pre-judge the lady's actions. She's someone very special. Besides—" He took a calming breath, the words difficult for him. "—nothing happened."

The expression on Blaine's face clearly said he didn't believe a word Dennis had said. He turned and walked out of the office, leaving a slightly shaken Dennis to ponder the true depth of Blaine's feelings for Meg.

Blaine went immediately to his office. He had talked to Harry earlier that day and confirmed that the erroneous information had made the circuit. There remained no doubt about the source of the information leak. He walked up to Emily's desk, stopped, and stared at her.

She looked up from her work. "Yes, Mr. Reeves? Is there something you require?"

"Come into my office. I want to talk to you." He closed the door and indicated a chair. "Sit down, Emily."

Half an hour later, Blaine opened the door. Red, puffy eyes peered out from Emily's ashen face, and she walked with her head slightly bowed.

"I am so terribly sorry, Mr. Reeves. I didn't know." She pulled herself together as they walked out of his office. With her back straighter, her head held higher and her prim businesslike manner in place, Emily continued to speak. "I know it will not make up for the damage I have caused, but you will, of course, have my resignation effective immediately."

"It's not necessary for you to resign, Emily. In fact"—a slight grin tugged at the corners of his mouth as he fought to keep what he knew was a devious glint from showing—"we might be able to turn this to our advantage. When Robert calls again, act as if nothing has happened. Agree to another date, then let me know. Do you think you can handle that without making him suspicious?"

For the first time since he'd told her what Robert had been doing, her mouth formed into a genuine smile, a combination of relief and pleasure. "Oh yes, of course. Thank you, Mr. Reeves. Thank you so much. I really don't want to leave this position. I enjoy working here and have the utmost respect for you."

He put his arm reassuringly around her shoulders. "Don't worry. It's going to be okay."

He gave her shoulder an extra pat, then started down the hall. He had several things to do and first on his list was a meeting with his Vice President of Finance. Ignoring the elevator, he took the stairs to the third floor. Two hours later, he returned to his office.

Emily immediately spotted him. "Oh, Mr. Reeves. Thank goodness you're still here. I was afraid you had gone for the weekend. Robert rang a bit ago. He wants to have dinner with me this evening. I told him I couldn't talk right then. He's supposed to ring me back at half past five. Did I do that properly?"

Blaine looked at his watch. It was five-fifteen. "You did it perfectly, Emily. Now, tell him that you have some last-minute details to deal with at work and it will be more convenient for you to meet him at the restaurant."

Emily followed his instructions and made the

arrangements with Robert, then notified Blaine of the results. When the time arrived, Blaine drove her to the restaurant. She was seated at the table where she waited for Robert.

She wrung her hands as her uncertain gaze darted nervously about the room. Blaine occupied the next table, seated close enough to hear Emily and Robert talking but with his back to the table so Robert wouldn't be able to see his face.

"Robert just arrived, Mr. Reeves."

Robert smiled as he approached her table. "Emily, how good to see you again." He seated himself next to her and signaled for the waiter's attention. "Let me order a bottle of wine for us. Have you had a chance to look at the menu?"

"Robert, there's someone here I would like you to meet." She gestured past his shoulder. "Robert Templeton this is Blaine Reeves, the owner of Pendragon Publishing."

Robert slowly turned around in his chair. His face went slack, and his eyes filled with apprehension as he looked up at Blaine's imposing six-foot two-inch frame towering above him. Blaine smiled at his secretary. "Thank you, Emily. William is outside in the limo. He'll see that you get home safely. I'll see you at the office on Monday."

Blaine turned a menacing look toward Robert as he seated himself in Emily's chair. "If I ever hear of you or anyone associated with Sir Geoffrey anywhere near my people again, I'll see that you pay dearly for it." Blaine gave him one last hard look that almost sent a visible shiver down Robert's spine. "It's bad enough that you've tried your underhanded business tactics on me, but that's business, and I'm equipped to deal with it. But it's unconscionable that you've toyed with Emily's affections and emotions in such a cold, callous, and cruel manner."

Then he turned and slowly walked toward the restaurant door.

****

When Emily had emerged from the restaurant into the parking lot, William immediately intercepted her, took her elbow, and gently guided her toward the limo. He held the car door open for her. "Emily, permit me to drive you home."

Tears welled in her eyes. She had behaved so shamefully. She had betrayed the trust her employer had placed in her. She tried to stop the sob in her throat but was not successful. She didn't want William to see her cry. She was too embarrassed to even look at him.

William handed her a clean handkerchief. His awkward manner could almost be called shy, as if he wasn't quite sure how to proceed. He hesitantly placed his arm around her shoulder in an offer of comfort. "Here, Emily. Please don't cry. That bounder isn't worthy of your attentions."

Emily looked up at William as she dabbed at her eyes. "I feel such a fool."

"You're much too fine a lady for the likes of him." His words faltered, making it obvious that he didn't have much experience in the social graces or with women. "Emily...I...uh, would you allow me to escort you to dinner this evening?"

She looked down at the ground, too embarrassed to make eye contact with him. "That's very gracious of you, William, but I'm sure you must have plans of your own.

You don't need to feel obligated. I'll be okay."

"I don't have any plans. I would be honored if you would consent to be my dinner companion...my guest for dinner."

She looked up at him and saw the sincerity on his face. "Do you really want to have dinner with me?"

"Very much so. I've often wanted to ask you to dine with me, but...well, I don't have much experience in these matters. I can't afford to take you to this type of establishment, but I do know a nice, quiet neighborhood restaurant that you might enjoy. You're a very nice person, Emily. I...I like you very much."

Emily offered a shy smile. "Thank you, William. I consider it a privilege to have dinner with you. I...I like you, too."

****

Robert Templeton sat across the desk from Sir Geoffrey, silently enduring the angry tirade. Sir Geoffrey's lips drew into a thin line of displeasure as his beady-eyed gaze drilled into Robert. "This is personal. Some upstart interloper American can't do that to me. What new projects does he have under way? Anything critical?"

Robert nervously cleared his throat before speaking. "There is a travel book that seems to have a very tight production deadline. It's the first in a series of travel books. He's imported a freelancer from the States to write and photograph it. I've looked into her credentials. She's very talented."

Sir Geoffrey's look softened slightly as he rubbed his long thin fingers across his pointed chin. "What else?"

"Well, I think our best approach on the travel book

would be through Dennis Mallory. He's going to be the key as to whether the book will make the publication date."

"No!" The suddenness of Sir Geoffrey's retort startled Robert. He shot a questioning look at his employer.

"We'll bypass Mallory. That's not our best avenue. We'll try the girl directly. She's an American freelancer, so she doesn't have a personal stake in any of this. With Americans, it's always about the money. We'll be able to buy her off. She'll be the easiest approach. Find out where she's staying."

****

Meg rose early Saturday morning, just before daybreak. She had spent a very restless night. Turmoil and anxiety kept her tossing and turning, as attested to by the tangled mess of sheets and blankets on the bed.

She stood at the window sipping her coffee while looking out over Hyde Park shrouded in gray fog. What had she gotten herself into? Blaine had been right about Dennis. And now, she would have to be working with Dennis in the office for at least two days before leaving for the countryside. She had the weekend to get herself under control and back on the right track. The best path for her would be to spend the time writing the rough draft of the London section. Hopefully, that would lessen the time she actually needed to spend in the office with him.

Everything seemed to be closing in around her. She felt like a little girl who wanted to run away to the safety of her favorite hiding place, to escape from this terrible mess. She wanted to get as far away from both Blaine and Dennis as she could.

Only she was not a little girl anymore. An

involuntary sigh of despair escaped her throat. She was an adult who needed to conduct her business with maturity, which meant completing the assignment in her most professional manner. She took a deep breath and slowly exhaled. She stared out over the park a moment longer, then retreated to the bedroom.

Dressing warmly, she went for a walk through Hyde Park. She strolled along the path, her eyes downcast as she watched the misty fog swirl around her feet. The grayness of the early morning exactly matched her confusion over her conflicting emotions. She walked slowly, silently contemplating her situation. After passing the Prince Albert Memorial, she crossed the street to Royal Albert Hall, then returned to her hotel. She had not consciously resolved anything, but a new feeling of calm settled over her as if an unconscious decision had somehow been formulated.

A renewed sense of energy infused her as she sat at the desk in her suite and began to work on the rough draft. She wanted it completed as quickly as possible, which meant she needed to work on it all weekend. That suited her just fine. It would occupy her time and give her a legitimate excuse to turn down any invitations should either Blaine or Dennis call.

Meg set up her laptop computer, took out the notes she had made during the days of location photography, and went to work. The time passed quickly as she began formulating her thoughts and notes into the London chapter of the book according to the format Dennis had presented at their initial meeting. By late afternoon, she had a nearly completed first draft of the London chapter and was ready to start on the rewrite and self-edit.

The phone interrupted her concentration and

workflow.

"No, Blaine. I'm not available for dinner tonight. I'm not available for breakfast, lunch, or dinner tomorrow. You remember this travel book of yours? The reason I'm in London? I have a rough draft to do in order to meet your tight production schedule, and I'm diligently working on it this weekend."

"You have to eat sometime."

"I can eat and work at the same time right here in my room."

"You need a break." His voice remained upbeat as he made a blatant attempt to inject a light-hearted note into the conversation. "You can't work non-stop. Besides, eating while you work is a sure path to indigestion."

"I have work to do. I'll see you Monday morning at the office. I'm hanging up now." She disconnected from the call before he had an opportunity to say anything else.

Her trepidation concerning a possible phone call from Dennis had been unfounded. The rest of the weekend went smoothly and peacefully. By the time she went to bed Sunday night, she had the text of the London chapter ready for Dennis' perusal. It had been a very productive weekend without any interruptions other than the one phone call from Blaine.

Tomorrow morning, however, would bring the necessity of seeing both Blaine and Dennis. And she would need to work with Dennis in the office. She took a calming breath, but it didn't quell the mounting anxiety churning inside her. How had her life suddenly gotten so out of control? And more to the point, what could she do about it?

Chapter Seven

Meg arrived at the Pendragon offices at nine o'clock Monday morning. She was immediately escorted to Blaine's office. He quickly put aside the papers he had been studying and rose from his chair.

"Good morning, Meg." His attitude formal—not cool, but not friendly either.

"Good morning, Blaine." Their initial meeting had been in Dennis' office. This was the first time she had seen his office. She quickly surveyed her surroundings. The silence in the room made her uneasy. She felt compelled to say something—anything. "So...this is your office."

As soon as she had spoken the words she realized how stupid and inane they sounded. She studied the large, tastefully, and artistically decorated room. It had a warm, comfortable feeling. In addition to his desk and other office furniture, there was a couch and two easy chairs in an arrangement. Another corner contained a small conference table with six chairs.

Blaine watched Meg. She seemed much calmer and more relaxed than before. She wore a silk blouse and matching silk slacks, the same shade of emerald green as her eyes. Her hair framed her beautiful face, hanging almost to her shoulders. And around her neck hung the gold chain he had given her so many years ago. He took encouragement in the fact that, after ten years, she still had it in her possession. And of more importance, she had been wearing it every time he had seen her since her arrival in London.

He continued to stare at her, closely scrutinizing her every move—the fluid motion of her body as she walked, stooped to pick up things and look at them, the gracefully sensuous movements. Pangs of despair twisted his insides into knots. Had she been with Dennis over the weekend? Was that her real reason for turning down his dinner invitation? He tried to shove the upsetting thought from his mind but without much success.

She finally came to rest, seating herself across the desk from him. "Okay, Blaine, I'm here. Now, what is it I'm supposed to be doing?"

"All the pictures you shot last week need to be individually identified, grouped into location, and tied into the rough draft of that section of the book. When you've finished, Dennis can start going over them for selection. He has an unerring eye and a sixth sense for what works in these situations. Time is of the essence. We have a very tight deadline for getting everything to the printer if we're going to meet our release date."

Her eyes narrowed slightly. A flash of apprehension crossed her face at the mention of working with Dennis, a moment that just as quickly disappeared. He caught her gaze with a questioning one of his own, but she averted hers.

He continued, uneasy about the possibility of finding out things he really didn't want to know. "You, uh, said you were going to work on the rough draft over the weekend. How far along are you?"

"I finished it."

He felt as if a weight had been lifted from his

shoulder. That meant she really had spent the entire weekend working. He walked toward his office door. "If you'll follow me, I have an office set up for you down the hall."

He escorted her to the temporary office. "All your pictures have been downloaded from the memory cards you gave me when we finished the last location on Friday. We ended up with nine hundred and forty images. I've had a computer workstation set up for your use."

A spontaneous laugh escaped her throat. "Nine hundred and forty images? I had no idea I shot that many pictures."

He allowed a relaxed laugh. "It surprised me, too. You're going to have a busy couple of days with this."

He started to leave her office, then turned back toward her. "If you need anything, my extension is written on the pad next to the phone. Dennis is working on something else this morning. By this afternoon, when he's available, hopefully you'll be far enough along identifying the pictures that he'll be able to start." He shook his head as he looked at the computer screen covered with thumbnail images. "There's a mountain of work here. If you have any problems with the identification and classification program we use, give me a shout. I'll see you later."

Blaine returned to his office, leaving Meg to start on her work. He glanced at the clock on his desk—nine-thirty. Crista's flight would arrive in two hours. He had planned to pick her up himself but had some pressing business to handle. He reached for the intercom. "Emily, have William pick up Crista at the airport and take her to my place."

That would work out fine. It would give Crista the afternoon to unpack, get settled, and take a little nap if she felt the need after her flight. He turned his attention to the pile of paperwork on his desk, the top item being a restructuring of the Sinclair project. He quickly became buried in work.

It seemed as if it had only been minutes, but when Blaine looked up from the stacks of paper the clock read eleven forty-five. He stood up and stretched, then casually walked down the hall to Meg's office. "How's it going?"

She looked up from her work and gave him a slightly weary smile as she rubbed at her shoulders in an attempt to ease her tight muscles. "I've been sitting too long. I'm going to have to do a couple of laps around the desk."

"How about a break? What would you say to some lunch? I'm a little pressed for time, so it won't be anything very glamorous. There's a good place just down the street within easy walking distance. We can grab a quick bite."

She glanced at her watch. Her expression softened, then she gave him one of those dazzling smiles he so remembered. "What would I say to some lunch? I'd say *hello lunch*. I'm hungry, and I can sure use the exercise."

They walked down the street to a small pub and found a table in a quiet corner. He looked into her eyes, then reached out to smooth the hair away from her cheek. "I'm glad you wore your hair down. I like it this way."

"Thank you." Her gaze darted nervously around the pub as if seeking something to change the subject. "I hope the food gets here soon. I'm starved. There's something about sitting in an office staring at hundreds of pictures on a computer screen that makes me really hungry."

"Are you making a dent in it at all?"

"I hope to have all of them identified by the end of the day, including renaming each picture to correspond with a category rather than the numerical file name generated by the camera. If not today, sometime tomorrow morning at the latest."

Blaine looked up as the waitress brought their lunch. "Ah, our food has arrived. Just in the nick of time."

Their casual conversation as they ate belied the intensity with which he studied her. She had changed, not as uptight as she had been since her arrival, somehow more relaxed and calmer. He momentarily flashed on her with Dennis, but he quickly shoved the disturbing thoughts aside. Dennis said nothing happened between him and Meg. He had never known Dennis to blatantly lie to him. He wanted to believe it but didn't know what represented the truth—the word of a world class womanizer or the evidence of the tie he left behind. A necktie in itself was not proof of anything other than Dennis having been there. But what reason would there be for him to have removed it?

He glanced at his watch. Twelve-thirty. She started to gather her purse for the walk back to the office. "Sit tight. I need to make a phone call. I'll be right back."

Meg watched his confident, graceful stride as he headed across the room and outside, she assumed to keep from annoying the other customers with his phone call just as he had done at lunch the first day of the location shooting. So many doubts and concerns. But one thing she knew for sure—Blaine Reeves remained the most desirable man she had ever known. She reflected on the last hour. The lunch had been surprisingly nice, the atmosphere relaxed and casual compared to the previous week's tension. She could actually say today almost felt comfortable.

Almost.

"Meg?" His voice intruded into her thoughts, his sudden reappearance shaking her out of her trance-like concentration. "I'm sorry, I didn't mean to startle you." He sat down. "You looked like you were a million miles away. Anything you'd care to share?"

She looked into the depths of his eyes. She saw softness and caring. No pretenses, only honesty. A smile tugged at the corners of her mouth. "No, it's nothing. I was only thinking and remembering…thoughts from long ago."

He tentatively reached out and covered her hand with his. She tensed at the physical contact, then relaxed without pulling her hand away. He captured her gaze. "I've never stopped remembering. You mean everything to me."

The words seemed to have slipped out, almost as if he hadn't intended to say them out loud. It was not what she expected to hear. Ten years ago she had assumed he loved her as much as she loved him. His every action and gesture said so, even though he had never said the words. But that was then. He had abruptly and painfully proven her wrong. And now…

"I wish I could believe you, Blaine, I really do. I wish…" She turned her head, breaking eye contact with him. "The past is what it is. The past can't be changed." As she looked away, the tears welled in her eyes. She quickly blinked them away, hoping he hadn't noticed.

They sat in silence. He turned her hand palm up and

slowly laced their fingers together. The warmth of his touch flowed through her veins and enveloped every fiber of her existence like a loving caress rather than a sexual surge.

"We have to talk, Meg. Let's go back to your hotel where we can have some privacy without the wagging tongues in the office."

Meg looked at him in genuine surprise. "I thought you had a very busy afternoon, and I know I have lots of work to do. Besides, isn't Dennis expecting me right after lunch?"

Blaine held her hand tighter. "I just called Emily. I told her to clear my calendar for the afternoon and tell Dennis you won't be ready for his help until tomorrow. Please Meg…we need to talk."

She silently regarded him for a moment. He'd been right about Dennis. She searched his eyes and face for some hint of an ulterior motive. She saw only open honesty and caring. Her words were hesitant, not sure of where any of this would take her. "Okay, I guess it will be all right as long as you're aware that you're keeping me from my work." She shot him a quick warning look. "But just to talk. That's all."

As they entered Meg's suite, she kicked off her shoes while he closed the door. He smiled and slowly shook his head. "You never could stand wearing shoes a minute longer than you had to."

She looked at the shoes resting on the floor. "I guess you're right. I've been kicking off my shoes as soon as I got home for as long as I can remember." She looked questioningly at him. "You remember that from way back then?"

Blaine looked lovingly into her eyes. "I remember

everything from *way back then*."

"So do I." A sob caught in her throat as she dropped her gaze to the floor. "And most of all, that one horrible day." Her voice was so soft as to be almost inaudible.

She tried to dismiss the sadness and shove the pain aside. Taking a bottle of wine from the bar, she poured two glasses and carried them to the table. She sat down in one of the chairs, purposely avoiding the sofa. He sat in the chair next to her. Her panic started as a small tickle, then quickly escalated. He was too attractive, too near, too desirable, and too dangerously tempting. Agreeing to this had not been a good decision.

She composed her tautly stretched nerves and tried to assume a more businesslike presence. "What is it you wanted to talk about that couldn't be said at the office?"

"I want to talk about us. I want to talk about us being together. I know you still have feelings for me. We couldn't have made love with such passion if it was only sex for the sake of sex, as you said, one for old time's sake." His gaze never wavered, his eyes revealing open, honest adoration.

The sting of her hurt burned her eyes. "That was all such a long time ago. Times have changed, people change. You say you've changed. Perhaps I've changed, too. You don't really know me anymore. I once believed everything you said, everything you did. I believed in you. I believed in *us*." Meg's voice softened as she choked on the emotion of her words. "Back then, I truly believed there was such a thing as *us*. Then you taught me a hard lesson, but a lesson I learned well. You taught me not to believe in such silly fairy tales. I was a naïve young girl back then." Her voice dropped to a nearly inaudible whisper. "And now, I'm not."

Would she ever be able to trust him with her love again? Would she ever be able to fully trust anyone?

A shudder moved through Blaine as he thought of the possibility of Meg and Dennis making love, even though he had to take at least some responsibility for it. He had practically pushed her into Dennis' arms in his over-zealous efforts to protect her. Dennis said nothing happened. He wanted to believe it even though Meg all but admitted it when she said she had changed, that she wasn't the person he knew. Were his fears driving him to jump to crazy conclusions? He couldn't get his mind wrapped around the notion. His emotions swirled around inside him, erratically darting here and there, totally out of his control.

His insides churned in turmoil, and his stomach twisted in hard knots of anxiety. Whether Meg and Dennis did or didn't have sex—he could no longer handle the notion of referring to it as them making love—it didn't change the way he felt about the only woman he had ever loved. About the only woman he would ever love. His life had no meaning without her.

He scooted his chair closer to hers. Desperation raged inside him. "What has happened in your past doesn't matter…if there is or has been someone else. Everything prior to right now is history and doesn't count."

Her entire demeanor changed as she looked at him in an almost defiant way. "The past doesn't count? Well, that's very magnanimous of you. What you did to me doesn't matter? And you graciously forgive me for whatever it is you imagine I might have done, no matter how terrible it is?"

He winced at her sarcasm. "I didn't mean for it to

sound like that. I just meant that you are a very desirable woman and surely there have been men in your life over the last ten years. There's no reason for me to assume you've been celibate."

"I see. And conversely, there's no reason for me to assume you've been celibate. Is that the way it goes? You've had your share of women…including your affair while we were still together—before you walked out on me—but suddenly none of that matters anymore?"

Blaine fought to maintain his calm and perspective. "No, that's not what I said, Meg." He looked at her as his annoyance pushed at him. "You're deliberately baiting me, twisting my words. All I said, and all I meant, was that up until this point you existed and I existed. From now on there will be us."

Meg looked at him for a very long moment as she turned the words over in her mind. "The past has been you and it's been me, but now you think it should be us? I had foolishly believed it was *us* ten years ago, but you dramatically demonstrated how wrong I was. What makes this time different? Why should I believe you now? How do I know if you're talking a lifetime or *us for the time being* until something better comes along to grab your attention?"

"Stop it, Meg! Stop playing devil's advocate. I want us to start over again, a new beginning. I want to change the past."

"Unless you own a time machine, the past cannot be changed. It is what it is." Her words were flat. The statement had been made without any emotion attached to it.

"Stop throwing semantics at me. You know what I mean."

"All right, you have no past, and I have no past. Yesterday doesn't exist. Here we are, brand new. Now, what do we do? What do you want from me, Blaine?" She blinked away the moisture forming in her eyes. "What is it you really want? What is all of this about?"

Blaine's mind darted from thought to thought. Her attitude genuinely confused him. "You're building a wall between us. I can feel it. It's growing brick by brick as we're talking. You're building a wall to hide behind. Please don't do this." He looked at her with an increasing sense of panic. "Building walls never solved anything. Don't shut me out."

"You mean don't shut you out the way you abruptly shut me out of your life ten years ago?"

An odd combination of frustration, panic, and anger roiled inside him. "Are you ever going to let us get beyond that? Are we going to continue to live in the past, unable to move forward? Forever allowing the past to control our lives? Denying any hope for a future?"

His words startled Meg, but they spoke the truth. That was exactly what she had been doing without realizing it, building a protective façade where she could retreat. A safe haven where she could hide from what she feared.

She looked at him, silently pleading for some kind of clarity to ease her confusion. "Tell me what you want, Blaine? What do you really want?" Despair filled her voice and surrounded her words. "Is it forgiveness to ease your conscience? Some sort of absolution? Ten years is a long time. Not once during those ten long years did I hear from you. You walked out on me and never looked back. Surely, you've been able to deal with your feelings and resolve your issues about that by now.

You've had a decade to deal with it."

She paused a moment to collect her thoughts. "You walked out on me without any problem or even a look back, totally betraying the trust I had placed in you. And I never knew why. I never knew what I had done to drive you away. For ten years, I didn't know if you were dead or alive. Why has it become such a big deal for you now? I'm seriously confused. I don't know what you want from me. You say you want us to be together. You manipulated and schemed to get me here. Now, what is it you want? Please tell me. No games. No pretty words or flowery speeches. And most of all—no empty promises."

She took a steadying breath. "No more lies, Blaine. Just give it to me in plain English so I can understand what you're talking about, so there won't be any confusion or misunderstanding. Don't tell me what you think I want to hear. Just tell me the truth for a change. That's what I want to hear."

"I want you, Meg. I want you, body and soul. I want you, mind and being. I want you to be part of me just as I want to be part of you. I want us to be together always."

"I've heard those words from you before. Why should I believe this is any different than when you said them the first time?" She couldn't hide the hard edge that clung to her words or the pain that lived in her heart.

He cupped her face in his hands, looked into her eyes, then leaned forward and brushed his lips lightly against hers. "I don't know what to say that will make you believe me. All I can do is ask you to please trust me again. Please…just one more time."

She closed her eyes. Her defenses slipped away as her resolve melted, and she was helpless to prevent it.

"Oh, Blaine. I want to believe you, I really do. But how can I? How can I ever trust you again? Trust you with my heart?" She opened her tear-filled eyes and once again searched his face for any hint of betrayal and deceit. "I thought I was going to literally die when you walked out on me. It took me a long time and all the strength I could muster to pull myself together and get on with my life, to build a future of my own, one without you. I don't think I could survive that kind of emotional devastation a second time."

He leaned forward and brought his mouth to hers, bestowing a kiss filled with incredible feeling and tenderness. She returned his kiss as she slowly put her arms around his neck. A tidal wave of emotion welled inside her as they sat at the table locked in each other's embrace. The sun finally broke through the gray gloom of the foggy day. A bright beam streamed in through the window, falling across their faces, picking up the golden highlights of Meg's hair.

He rose from his chair, bringing her to her feet with him. He looked lovingly into her eyes as he twined his fingers in her silky hair. He nuzzled her neck and whispered, "Megan, I want to make love to you. Regardless of what you said, the other night happened, and it can't be erased. It was real and very intense. I want to make love to you again...today, tomorrow, and every day for the rest of my life."

Thousands of emotions and sensations raced through her. She closed her eyes and tried to center herself, but all her attempts to focus landed on her burning desire for Blaine. She could not deny her need to once again have his naked body next to hers. Sex between them had always been hot and passionate, but that didn't mean he felt the same love she had been carrying around inside her all these years.

They walked toward the bedroom, his arm around her shoulders and her arm around his waist. When they reached the bedroom, she turned her face to him. He slowly unbuttoned her blouse as he claimed her mouth. A hot bolt charged through her as their tongues danced together and twined in a seductive rhythm.

Her breathing quickened. Her pulse raced. Suddenly, her clothes seemed too restrictive. A moment later, they landed on the floor. Blaine pulled the condom packets from his pants pocket, the ones he had taken from the locked drawer in his office desk before they went to lunch—again, an action based solely on wishful thinking rather than assumption—then the rest of his clothes quickly joined hers in a pile on the carpet.

She sensually ran her hands across the hard planes of his muscular chest. The feel of his bare skin beneath her fingertips sent a tingling sensation rippling through her body.

Blaine sucked in a deep breath and held it for a moment before slowly exhaling. Her mere touch was magic to him, sending his desires skyrocketing. He wanted her, all of her, again and again. In every way possible. For as long as possible.

Forever.

His breath caught in his lungs, and his heart pounded. His legs trembled until he finally fell backward onto the bed. He looked at her through half closed eyes. His erratic breathing increased as he took in her beauty. His desire for her coursed hot through his veins.

She had been able to propel him to places no other woman ever had, made him reach heights of ecstasy beyond what he believed possible. What had once been so familiar came back to him with the full intensity of the first time they had made love. He pulled her on top of him and again captured her mouth with heated fervor, his arousal fully extended. He ran his fingers across the curve of her bottom cheeks, and she responded by working her hand between their bodies so she could stroke his erection.

"Megan..." The words almost impossible for him to force out. "If you don't release me from your grasp, I won't be worth a damn for the rest of the day." She tilted her head to the side and shot him a quizzical look, followed by a teasing grin tugging at the corners of her mouth. "What's the matter? Was I doing it wrong?"

His words came out as a raspy whisper. "You know better than that."

"Or maybe you're just getting old."

"Old?" He tugged on her hand, a sexy grin playing across his lips.

She was everything he had ever wanted, everything he would ever want. A quick flash of memory darted through Blaine's mind, a memory of the first time they had made love. He told her he would never hurt her. He had asked her to trust him, and she had. Would he ever have that type of unconditional trust from her again?

They made love all that afternoon. Again and again, they abandoned themselves to their desires until totally spent. Skin glistened with beads of perspiration, arms and legs tangled, bodies exhausted. Outside the windows, a kaleidoscope of colors burst forth from the setting sun, streaking across the sky in a glorious explosion.

Meg snuggled her body against Blaine's warmth,

her back resting against his chest. He wrapped his arms around her, kissed her ear, and nuzzled the side of her neck. She responded to his tender touch with a sexy moan of delight in defiance of her body being satiated from the intense sex they had already shared. Her thoughts, however, remained a tangled mass of confusion.

For the second time since her arrival in London, they had made love with so much passion that it left her drained even though she knew it would never be enough. How she had missed his touch, his bare skin against hers, the exquisite pleasure he never failed to provide.

But what kind of problems had she created for herself?

By no stretch of the imagination could she pretend this magic had been an isolated incident, just an idle afternoon of casual sex. They had made love with an intensity that surpassed their lovemaking of just a few days ago. What kind of commitment did that signify? Or did it signify any type of commitment at all? He said he wanted them to be together. Well, for the past few hours they had certainly been *together*.

Now what?

He interrupted her thoughts with a soft whisper. "Meg...are you awake?"

She pulled back and looked at him in wonder. "You're not trying to tell me you actually have that much energy left, are you? I, for one, am deliciously exhausted."

He laughed, a low sexy laugh. "I didn't think I did, but this fine fellow"—he thrust his fully extended erection against her leg—"tells me differently."

"You're incorrigible."

He looked at her with loving sincerity. "The truth is I simply can't get enough of you. Oh, Megan, I don't want us to ever be apart again."

A troubled look crossed her face as she sat up. He reached to pull her back next to him, but she quickly slipped out of bed, evading his grasp. Her unexpected action surprised him. He looked up at her standing next to the bed, her eyes filled with confusion and wariness.

"I think you should go now." She spoke in a voice barely above a whisper. "I have a lot to think about, and I can't do it if you're here. You cloud my judgment."

He reached out and took her hand. "Come home with me, Meg. Now…tonight."

She gave his hand a little squeeze. "I can't. I have to sort out what's going on here. I never intended for this to happen. When I agreed to stay and finish the assignment, I never thought I'd ever allow you to get this close to me again. Yet here I am. Here we are."

He propped himself up on one elbow as he pulled her closer to him. A soft moan escaped her lips. A shiver ran through her body. She closed her eyes. "Please don't do that. I can't think when you do that."

He held her tighter.

"Please, Blaine…I…I can't think." Her resistance quickly dissolved as he pulled her onto the bed.

An hour later, she lay asleep in his arms. Outside, the day had turned into night and the lights of the city glowed across the horizon. He listened to her steady breathing. Crista had been at his apartment for several hours with no idea where he was or why he hadn't returned home. He had turned off his phone so he wouldn't be interrupted, which meant she hadn't been able to reach him. He didn't want to disturb Meg just to tell her he needed to leave, but he certainly didn't want to simply go while she slept. The last thing he wanted was for her to wake up and find only a note.

He carefully reached past her toward the phone on the nightstand. He dialed his home number. "Crista, I'm sorry to be late."

"Blaine, where are you? I called your office hours ago. Emily said she hadn't seen you since you and Meg left for lunch. I tried your cell phone, but it went straight to voice mail. I was about to call in Sherlock Holmes to track you down. I was beginning to suspect you'd pushed your luck too far with Meg, that she'd done you in."

He allowed a soft chuckle as he looked at Meg's sleeping body. She had done him in all right, in the most glorious way. "I should be home soon. I'm sorry to keep you waiting. Bye." He replaced the phone then saw Meg's eyes open as she watched him.

"Who was that?"

"Crista. She arrived today and is at my place. I was just telling her I'd be home soon."

"Crista is in town? What's the occasion?"

He spoke hesitantly, carefully measuring his words to keep from revealing his true motives for inviting his sister to stay with him. "She just went through a difficult divorce from Jack. She was in serious need of a change of scenery, to get away from her surroundings."

"I'm sorry to hear about that. Was it a sudden thing, or had it been coming on for a while?"

"It's the smartest thing she's done in quite some time. It was way past due." He gently stroked Meg's cheek with his fingertips and looked into her eyes. "I'd better get home. Crista has been at my place since about one o'clock. I'm afraid I'm being a rather neglectful host." He brushed his lips against hers, then captured her mouth with a passionate kiss.

She laughed as she pulled away from him. "You're not going to get home that way." She slid out of bed. "Come on, I'll race you to the shower."

She started for the bathroom with Blaine taking his time following her, his eyes riveted to the fluid motion of her body and graceful sway of her hips.

Chapter Eight

Blaine finally arrived home to find Crista sitting at his bar sipping a glass of wine. Even though she was eight years older, the family resemblance could not be denied—the same basic facial structure, the same eyes, although Crista's were more of an intense sky blue, her blonde hair a shade or two lighter than Blaine's sandy-colored hair.

She eyed him carefully. "I'm not sure where you've been or what you've been doing, but you certainly don't look like you've been suffering. That's without a doubt the most complete look of total satisfaction I've ever seen on a man's face."

The slight heat of embarrassment flushed his cheeks.

"Let me guess. You and Meg made up? You won't need my spying services after all?"

At the mention of the word *spying,* his mind moved back into the current reality. "I'm having trouble with the use of that word. I'm not trying to spy on Meg. I just want to protect her and make sure she's okay." A slight smile of satisfaction curled the corners of his mouth. "However, since I talked to you, things have changed. You're right. I've been with Meg since lunch." He paused, momentarily lost in thought. "The last several hours have been truly magical."

A frown wrinkled his brow. "She's still afraid I'll

hurt her again. I don't know how to convince her that I wouldn't..." The memory of what he had done welled inside him. "That I *couldn't* allow her to be hurt again, not by anyone else and definitely not by me."

He struggled to regain his composure, then continued. "And therein lies the problem, and the problem's name is Dennis Mallory. He set his sights on Meg. You know Dennis—the world's champ at fast-talking them, bedding them down, then moving on. In fact, he's already worked his wonders on her. I know he seduced her the other night. I found his necktie on the floor of her hotel room. When I confronted him, he claimed nothing happened, but I don't believe him. When I casually asked Meg about her dinner date with Dennis, she turned twelve shades of guilty and stammered that they ended up not going to dinner. You don't have to be a rocket scientist to figure that one out. Dennis is too damn slick for his own good."

Crista laughed. "Really, Blaine. Don't you think you might be jumping to conclusions? Meg wasn't a promiscuous woman, and I'm sure she hasn't changed her core value system during the last ten years. That's not her style. She wouldn't be casually sleeping around with someone she had just met. Besides, if Dennis told you nothing happened, why do you assume he's lying? Does he routinely lie to you? Have you caught him in several lies?"

"You don't know Dennis when he turns on the charm. I've watched him in action. For some reason, women find him irresistible. He never has to take no for an answer because no one ever tells him no."

"Well, baby brother of mine, that's not exactly true. I, too, have always found Dennis to be quite charming and very attractive. I've enjoyed his company on many occasions."

Shock slammed through Blaine. "Crista…are you saying—"

She held up her hand to stop him in mid-sentence. "Before you jump to even more absurd and ludicrous conclusions than you already have, hear me out. Dennis hit on me, and I rebuffed him with my wedding ring. He always accepted my no as a valid answer and never tried to talk me into anything or take advantage of me in any way." A twinkle lit Crista's eyes as she held up her left hand and wiggled her bare ring finger. "Of course, now, I have no wedding ring…"

She gave Blaine a smile and a wink. "I'll tell you what. Rather than spying on Meg, I'll spend my time keeping Dennis busy for you."

He eyed her suspiciously. "You know, sometimes I'm not sure when you're kidding and when you're not."

"What makes you think I'm kidding? I'd much rather do that than have to wrestle with my conscience over spying on Meg because of your wild unfounded assumptions." Crista turned very serious as she continued, leveling a stern look at her brother. "Not only did you abruptly walk out on that lady without even a hint to her of what was to come, you made no attempt to contact her during the ensuing decade. You have no right to try to control her life or question her actions. She's an adult who can do as she chooses and with whom she pleases. She doesn't need your permission. She doesn't owe you anything, least of all an explanation. I really do believe you're very serious in your desire to have her back. The two of you were meant for each other. You should have married her ten years ago. I hope you can win her back, but it's not going to be easy. You hurt her very deeply and callously betrayed the very core of her trust, something totally out of character for you. It's certainly understandable that she's afraid to trust you again."

Crista rose from the bar stool, walked over to the large living room windows, and stared out at the river and the lights on Tower Bridge. She finally turned back toward Blaine. "Judging by that satisfied look on your face when you walked in the door, I assume you and Meg spent the last several hours making love. I guess that's a start. But remember, that's only the physical side of a relationship. It can't replace the trust you destroyed. Regaining that trust will take longer if it happens at all. You might have to be content with making love to her, knowing that she will never again really give herself to you fully, never again give you her trust and her heart."

Utter despair mixed with deep emotional pain as he nodded. "I know."

"I noticed the new addition to your living room. When did you do the painting?" Crista asked, changing the subject.

"I did it shortly after Meg arrived in London."

"Has she seen it?"

"No, you're the only one who's seen it. You're the only one who has been here since I painted it."

"You should show it to her. The love you feel for her simply leaps off that canvas. It's the best thing you've ever done, without a doubt. Tell me, does she know about the two photographs of hers that you bought?"

"No, to the best of my knowledge she has no idea who bought them." Desperation crept in. "You've got to help me, Crista. I'm at the end of my rope. I don't know what to do about Dennis and Meg. Every time I think of him having sex with her, my insides twist into knots. I clench my teeth so hard it makes my entire jaw ache."

"Having sex? That certainly sounds a lot more impersonal than making love."

He slowly shook his head. "To think of it any other way somehow gives it legitimacy. Besides, with Dennis it's always impersonal...nothing more than sex."

Crista studied Blaine's face. He had always been very confident and in control. She had never seen him so at a loss about what to do or how to proceed. She had no doubt about his state of mind, of being so deeply in love with Meg and so frustrated by the situation that he could barely function.

She sat on the couch next to him, putting her arm protectively around his shoulders just as she had done when he was a little boy and she was a teenager. "I don't know what I can do, but I'll help any way I can. I want to see the two of you back together. You'll never find a woman more perfect for you than Meg."

He smiled and put his arms around her, giving her a grateful hug and a kiss on the cheek before grabbing her empty wine glass and carrying it to the bar. He poured her another glass and one for himself.

Crista cautiously changed the direction of their conversation, knowing she was about to embark on a very touchy subject. "I talked to Dad before I left New York. I told him I was coming here for a visit. He asked about you." She tried to determine his reaction. "Why don't you let bygones be bygones and give him a call? He's mellowed a lot in the last few years. I know he's real proud of your success. Please, give him a call."

Blaine's face turned hard. "He let me know exactly what he thought about me after Mom died." His voice contained all the bitterness he had carried inside him for nearly twenty years, since he was fifteen years old. "He wanted Mr. Macho for a son, someone who would go to the fights with him, someone he could take hunting. What he had was a son who liked art and played tennis."

Painful memories flooded his mind. "Do you know what he once told me? I was fifteen years old, but I vividly remember every word as if it happened yesterday. He was sitting in the living room in his usual drunken stupor. He said, 'Boy, all that stuff you do…the painting and the tennis… That's all sissy stuff. Are you queer, boy? Is that your problem? Have you ever had sex with a girl? You're old enough now, boy, to know what life's all about.' "

Slowly, a bittersweet smile tugged at his lips.

Crista cocked her head and raised her eyebrows. "What's with that expression? What are you thinking?"

"Remembering more than thinking. My drunken father is asking me if I'm gay and telling me what I need is a girlfriend. Little did he know that I was experiencing a very active sex life, especially for a fifteen-year-old, and had been for about three months."

A broad grin spread across Crista's face. "You're kidding. At the young age of fifteen? I never suspected. Tell me—who was she?"

"No one knew about it. She was an *older woman* of seventeen. I may have been only fifteen, but I was smart enough to keep my mouth shut and not mess up a good thing by bragging about it." He shot her a sly wink. "And I'm still smart enough to keep my mouth shut."

She shook her head. "I always thought I knew you,

that we never had any secrets. Apparently, I was big time wrong."

Anger once again clouded Blaine's mind. "And that drunken bastard is telling me that being a real man is cheating on your wife, not showing her any respect, just giving her an occasional tumble to keep her happy while you're running around town chasing anything in a skirt."

She spoke slowly, as if carefully choosing her words. "He's changed. He really has. He took it very hard when Mother died. It sort of unhinged him for a while. He may have been crude, but deep down he really loved her."

"Of course, he took it hard." Blaine's voice spewed all the bitterness he felt toward his father. "Without Mom, he had no one to boss around, no one at his beck and call to act as his indentured servant. You were already married, and he had written me off as a lost cause. After seeing the way he treated Mom, I swore I'd never treat any woman that way." Blaine's voice softened. "My wife, any woman, would be treated with respect. My wife would be my partner. An equal in all ways."

"Then how do you justify leaving and attempting to control Meg?"

Stunned, it took a moment before he found his voice. "What are you talking about? I'm not trying to control her."

"No? You trick her into being in London, manipulate the circumstances to have her near you. Now that she's here, you want her to see only who you want her to see and go only where you want her to go. You even brought me here to make sure she behaves the way you want her to. That doesn't sound equal and respected to me. You're trying to force restrictions on someone you don't even have an existing relationship with, someone you haven't set eyes on in ten years. What would you call that?"

The true realization of his own actions, born from his desperation, seeped into his consciousness. "I'd call that reprehensible, truly intolerable behavior if I saw someone else doing it." He paused to compose the flood of emotion welling inside him. "She really does care for me. I know she does. I can feel it, and after this afternoon…"

"Has she told you so? Has she even said she forgives you?"

"Well, no."

"Then why do you think you have the right to try to control her? Because of what you want? What about what she wants and needs?"

Blaine didn't answer. Crista was right. She had always been his anchor and the voice of reason in stormy times. The silence hung heavily in the air for a long moment, then he composed himself and changed the subject. "Did you give up on me and finally raid my refrigerator, or are you still waiting for me to take you out to dinner?"

"One look at the inside of your refrigerator should answer that question. All the good stuff is gone." She stifled a yawn. "It's been a long day, and I'm really tired. I've already moved my things into the guest room and am all settled. I'll see you in the morning."

After giving him a kiss on the cheek, Crista went to the bedroom and closed the door. Blaine sat down on the couch and stared at the painting of Meg hanging above the fireplace. His love for her welled inside him. He continued to stare at the painting, lost in thoughts of the past and hopes for the future. He finally turned out the lights and went to bed.

****

Blaine woke early the next morning to a quiet apartment, noting Crista's closed bedroom door. He hurriedly took a shower, dressed for work, then left her a note saying to come to his office for lunch.

Seven o'clock that morning found him at his desk, trying to catch up on the paperwork he had abandoned the previous afternoon. When he had decided to start his own publishing company, all this executive paperwork had not been part of his plan. A smile curled his lips and his eyelids closed as he recalled just how he had spent yesterday afternoon. He may be facing a backlog of paperwork now, but it had certainly been worth it.

At eight o'clock, Dennis stuck his head in Blaine's office. "Hi. I just thought I'd check with you to see when Meg will be ready for me to start working with her on the London section."

Blaine eyed him suspiciously. "About midafternoon should be right."

Dennis gave him a breezy smile and a wave of his hand. "I'll be there." Then he disappeared down the hall to his office. Blaine returned his attention to his work.

"Your secretary isn't at her desk. Is it okay if I come in?"

Blaine looked up at the sound of Meg's voice. As soon as he set eyes on her, his entire spirit lifted. He came out from behind his desk and started to kiss her.

She immediately stopped him. "The wagging tongues in the office, remember?" She changed the subject. "How's Crista? I hope you didn't keep her waiting too long."

He put his arm around Meg's shoulders as he walked her into his office. "I can't speak for Crista, but as far as I'm concerned, it was worth every minute."

Her cheeks turned crimson, then the blush spread to the rest of her face. "That's not exactly what I was asking." He held a chair for her as she sat down. "Since I'll be leaving for the countryside in a couple of days or so, I hope I get the chance to see Crista while she's in town."

"She'll be here for about a month. This escape from her daily routine will do her a world of good, really recharge her batteries and get her going again. Besides, you'll only be gone for a few days, then you'll be back in town for a couple of days before you head out again. I know Crista's looking forward to seeing you. She was surprised when I told her you were here."

"I'll bet she was. In fact, I'm sure it was about the last thing she expected." Meg's voice dropped to almost a whisper. "I know it was definitely the last thing I expected." She stood and looked toward the office door. "Well, I'd better get down the hall. I have a lot of work to do."

****

Meg sat in front of her computer, working on identifying the rest of the pictures when a knock on the doorjamb of the open door interrupted her concentration. She turned and saw Dennis framed in the doorway.

A flash of uncertainty, combined with a heavy dose of anxiety, darted through her as she gave him a polite but businesslike smile. "Good morning."

Dennis gave her his standard sexy smile and walked across the office toward her. She stiffened as the wariness invaded her. He stopped halfway, his manner instantly changed from breezy to serious. "Meg, please. Don't look at me like that. I can't begin to tell you how badly I feel about what happened. I don't know what came over me. I promise you, it will never happen again. Forgive me?"

Meg wasn't sure how to respond to his apology. She wanted to believe him and put the unpleasant incident behind her. The book assignment dictated she work with him. Things would go much smoother and quicker without the strained tension that currently existed.

She studied him for a long moment. She saw the uncertainty in his eyes and the awkward way he shifted his weight from one foot to the other, a manner far removed from the confidence and easy charm he had exhibited from the moment she first met him. He continued to look at her rather than away. In addition to the uncertainty, she also saw a surprising honesty there.

He raised his right hand as if swearing an oath and gave her a pleading look, almost like a sad puppy dog. "Please? Forgive me?"

She couldn't stop the laugh that escaped her throat. "Okay, Dennis. Who can stay mad at that poor little puppy dog look? You're forgiven." Then she shot him a hard look. "I expect you to keep that promise."

"Thank you, Meg. That's one promise I'll never forget, one I'll always honor." He extended his hand.

She hesitated then tentatively reached out for it but drew back slightly before making contact with him.

"Now, now. I thought we were going to shake hands and be friends." He continued to hold out his hand.

She reached out again, and they shook hands.

"Well, luv, I must get back to my office. I have lots

to accomplish before we start on our project this afternoon. I'll see you later." He gave her a wink and smile before leaving her temporary office.

She returned her concentration to her work.

****

At eleven-thirty, Crista entered the building and went up the elevator. She exited at Blaine's floor and ran into Dennis—literally.

"Crista, what a marvelous surprise. When did you arrive in town?"

"Yesterday. Well, Dennis, you're looking marvelous, as usual. How's your love life been?"

"You know me. I hate staying home alone." He gave her a sexy smile and wink as he put his arm around her shoulders and walked down the hall with her. "What are you doing here, how long are you staying, and more importantly, when am I going to take you out to dinner so I can make yet another futile attempt at ravishing your body?"

She shot him a knowing grin. "How about dinner tonight?"

"I'd be honored. Are you staying at Blaine's flat?"

"Yes."

"Good. I'll collect you at seven. Is that okay?"

"That will be fine." Then she added, "Maybe we can even get a chance to discuss that *ravishing* you were talking about."

His face held a slightly perplexed expression as they arrived at Blaine's office. Emily smiled as she saw Crista. "Mrs. Franklin, how good to see you again. Go right in. Mr. Reeves is expecting you."

"Thank you, Emily. It's nice to see you again, too."

Dennis walked Crista to Blaine's door. "Look who

I found wandering around the hallway. I tried to tempt her with some chocolates, but she insisted on being brought directly to you." Dennis gave Crista a friendly little peck on the cheek. "So long, luv, see you later." He sauntered down the hall toward his office.

Blaine's lips curled in obvious disgust. "He never gives it a rest."

"Now, Blaine. You're viewing him from a slightly biased perspective."

"Oh?" The sarcasm seeped into his voice. "And what perspective would you suggest?"

She shot him a teasing grin. "A woman's perspective."

His expression said he wasn't amused. "I don't think I can manage that."

"I, personally, am very fond of Dennis. He is who he is. One day, he'll grow up and discover that the world is not his personal playground and all women are not his personal play toys. When that day comes, he's going to be really hurting for friends. My guess is he has hundreds, maybe even thousands, of acquaintances and even casual friends but no real friends."

Blaine looked at her. He could see she had merely stated what she thought, describing what she saw and knew of Dennis. She had always been able to get to the bare essence of a person without any trouble. She had an uncanny ability to be able to accurately read people and see them for what they really were. Her only major error in judgment had been marrying Jack Franklin.

Crista looked around the office as she sat down. "Do you have Meg here somewhere? I'd like to say hello, or will she be joining us for lunch?"

He reached for the phone and dialed an extension.

After a moment, he spoke. "How about some lunch?" He listened to Meg's reply. A hint of embarrassment heated his face as he lowered his voice. "No, honest. Only lunch. Crista is here, and she'll be joining us."

Crista interrupted. "Please, don't alter any personal plans on my account."

He raised his hand and gestured for Crista to be quiet. "Fine, why don't you come on down to my office as soon as you finish that, then we'll get something to eat. See you in a few minutes." He hung up the phone and turned back to Crista. "You really get a kick out of trying to embarrass me, don't you?"

She laughed at his irritation. "It's one of the few genuine pleasures of life that I have left to me." She eyed him knowingly. "If I were you and had a choice between spending a lazy afternoon making long, drawn-out passionate love with a beautiful woman or taking my older sister to lunch… Well, I'm afraid lunch and the sister would come in a distant second. But just try to figure out some people." She paused for a moment. "Seriously, if you and Meg would like to make some other plans, I'll bet I could get Dennis to take me to lunch."

"Don't be such a smart-ass. If I had better plans, I wouldn't have asked you to lunch in the first place. I'm not that dumb." They continued to banter genially until Meg arrived.

"Crista, it's so good to see you. It's been too long. You look great."

"Well, Meg, you've always looked great, but now you look positively radiant. I don't know what you've been up to lately, but whatever it is sure agrees with you." The two women exchanged an affectionate hug as

Meg gave Blaine an embarrassed look and Crista smiled knowingly.

The three of them left the office and went to lunch. They caught up on old times and talked about Crista's divorce and Meg's book assignment. After lunch, they walked back to the offices. Crista made the first move to break up their threesome. "I want to do some shopping, so I'll be running along."

"Okay, I'll see you at home later," Blaine replied.

"Only if you're there before seven. That's when Dennis is picking me up for dinner. Don't wait up for me. I assume I'll probably be out late. You know Dennis." She winked at Blaine, hugged Meg, then left them standing in front of the Pendragon Publishing office building.

"Crista and Dennis have the oddest relationship. They've been friends for eight years. They simply enjoy each other's company. Crista is probably the only woman Dennis knows that he doesn't constantly hit on. I think they genuinely like each other as people. For Dennis, that is a very foreign relationship to have with a woman."

Blaine looked at Meg and again saw what he had been interpreting as guilt. The recurring vision of Dennis and Meg in bed together popped into his mind. He quickly buried his mounting anger and pain as he changed the subject. "How are you coming with the project?"

"It's moving along very quickly. I should be ready for Dennis' help by three o'clock." She entered the office building through the door he held open for her. "It was good to see Crista again. How's she holding up with regard to her divorce? Was the split with Jack an amicable one? I sure hope everything works out okay for her. I've always been very fond of Crista."

"She'll be just fine. She's a very together lady. She and Jack had been estranged for quite a while, legally separated for the last six months. It just took her a little while to make the move to file for divorce. It's a pretty big step, especially when you've been married twenty-five years and have two kids. The oldest lives in Seattle, and the younger is away at college. She finally decided there wasn't anything about the marriage she wanted to try to salvage, that the inevitable couldn't be put off any longer."

Blaine brushed his fingertips against her cheek. "I think it's the best thing for her. Jack was really behaving like an ass, especially the last four years. I don't know if he was just going through some sort of prolonged mid-life crisis or what, but he was sleeping around and the younger the better. He didn't even have the courtesy to make a stab at discretion. Crista said the last one was only twenty-one years old, younger than their oldest son. Jack is forty-eight. I don't understand what gets into some guys. Jack had a terrific wife and family, and he didn't have enough sense to keep them."

She looked at him in disbelief. "You don't understand how that can happen? How someone can have a good thing and just throw it away without a second thought?" An edge of bitterness tinged her voice. "You seem to be suffering from a severe memory lapse."

He stopped walking and stared at her. The hurt he saw in her eyes left him shaken. "Oh, my God, Meg. I'm sorry. I didn't mean it like that."

He tried to determine the damage he had done with his careless remarks. She was again hiding her emotions.

Her beautiful green eyes went blank, holding no hint of what was going on behind them.

"I have lots of work to do. I'd better get back to it." She turned away and walked down the hall, leaving him staring after her.

Meg returned to her temporary office. She sat at the desk, staring out the window. Yesterday afternoon and evening with Blaine had been incredible, and now this. On two separate occasions since her arrival in London, they had spent many hours making love with an intensity she hadn't known in ten years. But that was physical. Was that all there would ever be? How could she ever trust him again?

She cleared her head, turned toward the computer, and resumed her work. After a couple of hours, she glanced at her watch. Three o'clock. She heard the knock at the open door and looked up to see Dennis standing at the doorway. He gave her his sexy smile and a wink.

"Are you ready for me?"

She extended a smile. "I am just about ready for you. Your timing is perfect." She looked into his eyes for a second longer, then returned her attention to the business at hand. "I've identified most of the pictures and put together the copy covering the London section of the book. Why don't you look at the rough draft while I finish up these pictures, then we can discuss what you want." She looked up at him, again revealing her dazzling smile. "Is that okay with you?"

"Sure, that will be fine."

Dennis moved across the office to the couch by the window and sat down but did not look at the material in his hands. He watched her at work. If he didn't know better, he would swear she was coming on to him. But, of course, that couldn't be, not after what happened the other night. Or could it? An unaccustomed confusion swirled around inside his head. Was she free for dinner?

Then he remembered his dinner engagement with Crista. Maybe Meg would be at her hotel, all alone, after he took Crista home. He felt a rush of excitement as he contemplated a second chance with Meg, but only if she was willing. No way would he repeat his deplorable behavior with her.

Suddenly that twinge hit him again. He dismissed it and turned his concentration to the work at hand.

He read her rough draft of the London section, making a few notations along the way, then set the sheets of paper on the table. "This is excellent, luv. You've expanded on the original concept in a very imaginative way. And what I saw of the pictures after they were downloaded into the computer system... They're incredible. I'm going to have a very difficult time narrowing down the selection, especially from so many images." He gazed across the room at her. "I'm very impressed, very impressed indeed."

"Thank you, sir. I'm very flattered."

He continued his steady gaze at her and added his sexy smile. "Oh? Is it some of that flattery you told me would go a long way with you?"

The crimson blush of embarrassment spread across Meg's cheeks, but her voice took on a hard edge. "That's not what I meant."

Dennis checked the time. Five-thirty. He wanted to run home to take a shower and change clothes before picking up Crista for dinner. He surveyed the clutter in the office, papers and pictures everywhere. "Well, luv, what would you say to our cleaning up this mess and calling it a day?"

"That sounds good to me. I am kind of tired. I feel like I've been sitting much too long."

"What kind of big plans do you have for the evening?"

"I don't have any plans. I thought I would stay in and do some more work on the book. Now that you've approved the draft, I want to get started on the rewrite and incorporate your suggestions."

"My corrections are minor. It shouldn't take you very long."

He picked up the last of the photo layouts and handed them to her. "May I give you a lift to your hotel? It's on my way."

"Thanks, but I'd rather walk. It's not really that far, and I can use the exercise."

He gave her a wink. "Don't wear yourself out. Save some energy for later." As soon as the words were out of his mouth, he realized they sounded too aggressive. To his relief, her eyes sparkled and she had an amused smile on her lips.

"You just never stop, do you?"

He allowed an almost shy smile, albeit it a genuine one, along with a shrug of his shoulders. "Sorry luv, just habit."

Meg gathered her things and left the office. As she passed Blaine's door, she noticed him buried in a sea of paperwork. Just as well. She needed some time alone to think without distractions. And Blaine Reeves was a major distraction.

She continued down the hall, passing the elevator in favor of the stairs.

Chapter Nine

"Dennis, come in. I'll just be a minute. Make yourself comfortable." Crista gestured toward the bar. "Feel free to fix yourself a drink. I'll be right back." She went into the bedroom, leaving him alone in the living room.

His gaze went immediately to the painting of Meg hanging above the fireplace. He stood staring at it for several minutes, mesmerized by the portrait.

"It's a beautiful painting, isn't it?"

He turned at the sound of Crista's voice. "It's…it's breathtaking. Where did it come from?"

"Blaine painted it."

"Blaine did this? I knew he was an artist, but I had no idea he was this talented."

"His artistic ability is how he supported himself here in London until he was able to get Pendragon off the ground, that and giving tennis lessons."

A soft chuckle escaped his throat. "I knew about the tennis. He's made me feel like a beginner on several occasions when he totally destroyed my confidence." He took another look at the portrait. "When did she pose for it?"

"She didn't. He painted it from memory shortly after Meg arrived in London. The emotions just leap off the canvas at you. Can you feel them? I can."

He continued to stare at the portrait a moment longer

before managing to force out a response. "Yes, so can I. They're very powerful feelings. He loves her very much, doesn't he?"

"Yes, he does…very much."

"Has Meg seen the painting?"

"No, she doesn't even know it exists."

Dennis paused awkwardly, then asked what had been on his mind constantly since the initial confrontation between Blaine and Meg that first day in his office. "Crista…" He turned toward her. "What happened between them? Something from a long time ago? Something that hurt her very deeply?"

She gave him a long piercing look. "Why do you want to know?" Her eyes narrowed as she watched him. "This isn't some casual thing you can meddle in for your own personal gain or amusement. Anyway, this is between Blaine and Meg. It's something they will have to deal with, work out between them if they can. And if they can't…" She brightened and changed the subject. "Come on, I'm starving." She shot him a teasing grin. "At which incredibly expensive restaurant will we be dining?"

He laughed. "I'll have to check my finances to see if I can afford anything more than fish and chips." He offered her his arm. As they left the flat, he glanced back at the portrait. A flood of emotion washed over him. He sensed all of Blaine's deep feelings for Meg. And now Blaine's anger when he found the necktie made sense.

Dennis and Crista enjoyed a leisurely dinner, talking comfortably as old friends would. She told him about her divorce and why it happened, about Blaine inviting her to London for a change of scenery. She talked about indecision concerning what she wanted to do with her life. He briefly mentioned his growing concern over his own lifestyle and his uncertainty as to how he could alter it without giving it up.

Suddenly, he stopped talking and looked at her. He flashed his sexy smile, more out of habit than any conscious thought. "You're far too comfortable to be with, luv. Pretty soon you'll have me pouring out my most private inner secrets and fears."

A spontaneous laugh escaped her throat, then her expression turned serious. "You're going to have to make some decisions. You can't have both sides of the coin. Either straighten up your act or prepare to grow old alone."

He studied her face. He didn't like what she said, but he knew she spoke the truth. Crista and Blaine were the only ones who had ever bothered to tell him things he really didn't want to hear. Everyone else let him slide through on his glib tongue and charm.

Crista cocked her head to one side and arched an eyebrow to question the odd expression covering his face. "What?"

He brushed her cheek with his fingertips, then rested his hand along the side of her face. A strange sensation quickly danced across her skin. His eyes looked deeply into hers.

"You know, Crista, you are really a very special lady. Jack is a fool for treating you that way. He didn't deserve you." He continued to hold her gaze. "He can sleep with every young woman in the whole of the United States, and it won't bring him any real satisfaction or happiness. He won't find whatever it is he's seeking." He dropped his hand back on the tabletop. "I know because I've been trying to do just that for all my adult life, and it doesn't work, not deep down, not where it really counts."

This was a side of Dennis she had never seen before, a deeply hidden, sensitive vulnerability. She put her hand on his arm and gave him a reassuring smile. "You don't suppose you're actually developing a conscience, do you? I realize it's a foreign concept, but you might find that you like it."

He snapped back to his old façade—his comfort zone—as he flashed one of his patented sexy smiles. "Bite your tongue." He leaned across the table and lowered his voice to a sensual whisper. "Or better yet, let me do it for you."

She smiled seductively as she squeezed his arm. "I bet that would certainly be *my* pleasure."

Her words and tone threw Dennis totally off balance, a situation very foreign to him. He didn't have the vaguest idea whether she was kidding or serious. The twinkle in her eyes seemed to have much more depth than he usually saw when she kidded with him. For the second time that day, he had been unsure about whether a woman had come on to him or was merely joking.

For the first time in his adult life, Dennis Mallory found himself engulfed in bewilderment and at a loss for words.

She gave him a warm smile. "Oh, Dennis. You should see your face."

He finally managed to stammer what he hoped didn't sound like incoherent babbling. "Crista, I don't know what's going on here. Are we having one of our usual conversations where I try to get you into bed and you tell me I'm being ridiculous?" He tried to swallow the anxiety that suddenly flooded his consciousness. "Or is there something more happening here?"

"Well, Dennis...bewilderment, confusion, even a little bit of vulnerability. This is a side of you I've never seen before." She gave him a very warm and inviting smile. "I like this side of you. It makes you a much more attractive man. I find it very appealing. Yes, indeed...*very* appealing."

Her steady gaze left him unnerved. He looked around the table, trying to find something to break the tension knotting in the pit of his stomach. He noticed her empty wine glass.

"Here, let me pour you some more wine." As he reached for the bottle, he clumsily knocked it over, spilling the little bit remaining on the table cloth. Heat rose in his cheeks as he took his napkin and tried to clean up the spill. The waiter rushed over to help, but Dennis quickly stopped him. "That's okay. Could I just have the bill?"

Dennis' embarrassment stayed with him as they left the restaurant. "I'm sorry about that. I'm not usually that clumsy. I don't know what happened to me back there."

He looked at her as he took her arm and brought her to a halt. He placed his hands on her shoulders and eyed her intently. "That's not true. I do know what happened to me back there. It was you. All the women I've had don't mean a thing to me. I've never had a woman talk to me as straight and honestly as you just did, as you always do."

He looked deeply into her bright blue eyes. Usually, when he looked into a woman's eyes, it was to gauge her response to his line. But not this time. His awakened reality embraced a new understanding and a deep sense of caring.

His anxiety level jumped up a notch. "Am I about to make a mistake here, Crista? If I'm starting something that I shouldn't, please tell me to stop."

He leaned down and gave her a tender kiss. Not one of his usual *of course I'll respect you in the morning now take off your clothes* type of kisses. This kiss conveyed tender feelings and caring.

She returned his kiss, brushing her tongue lightly against his lower lip. For the first time in more years than he could remember, he felt like a schoolboy embarking on a new adventure. He didn't know where it would take him, but he felt a rush of exhilaration at the prospect of the journey. He put his arm around her shoulders as they walked to the car.

Dennis and Crista drove back to Blaine's apartment. The windows were dark. He walked her to the door. "Blaine must not be home yet. Do you want to come in for a drink?"

Apprehension welled inside him. "No, I don't think I should." He put his hands on her shoulders and turned her to face him. "I don't want to make a mistake with you. I need to go home and sort this thing out. We've been good friends for eight years. I don't want to jeopardize that on one night of rash actions and wrong assumptions. If something is going to happen here, I want to know that we'll still be friends. Your friendship is very important to me. I have very few real friends."

She studied him for a moment. "That's what true relationships are about. Being friends usually comes first, everything else comes later. I know that's not the way you approach women. With you, sex comes first, and there's nothing more than that. But you should try the friend route. You'll see it really works." She opened the door, stepped inside, then turned back to him. "One last chance. Are you sure you don't want to come in?"

He looked into the living room, then back at her. "No, I don't think so." His face brightened. "Let's have dinner Friday night, then on Saturday we can drive out into the country for lunch. How does that sound?"

"That sounds delightful. I look forward to it."

He drew her to him and gave her another kiss, this one bordering on barely concealed passion. He pulled back and looked longingly into her eyes. That afternoon he had toyed with the idea of stopping by Meg's hotel room, his intentions definitely removed from business. In fact, his intentions were not even honorable. But now, that would not happen. Crista filled his thoughts. Confused thoughts. Thoughts he needed to sort out. "I'd better go while I still have the ability to walk to my car."

Crista watched as Dennis drove down the street. She closed the front door and went to her bedroom. A few minutes later, she snuggled under the covers, her thoughts layered one on top of the other. She had always found Dennis to be sexually enticing and physically attractive. But more than that, she had always liked him personally.

Right now, however, her desires were centered wholly on Dennis making love to her. She wanted him to whisk her away from the daily routine of reality and take her into a world of sensuality, a world where she could once again feel like a desirable woman, even if only for a little while.

The last year with Jack had taken its toll on her feelings of self-worth, of being an exciting sensual woman. Of even being moderately desirable. As Blaine said, she needed to recharge her batteries, but picking up strangers for a one-night stand did not fit her style. At forty-five years of age, she did not fit into the singles bar scene. The perfect solution to her specific situation? Dennis Mallory.

She smiled to herself as she envisioned their bodies seductively entwined. The kiss he gave her at the front door held so much promise. If that amount of heated passion could be conveyed by one kiss with him holding back, then Dennis unrestrained should be well worth the wait. She drifted off to sleep, sweet anticipation coloring her dreams.

****

Blaine had finally managed to get to the bottom of the pile of paperwork on his desk. Eight-thirty—it felt much later. Everyone else had gone home hours ago. He slowly stretched out his tall frame, trying to work out the kinks in his neck and back from being hunched over his desk too long. Owning a publishing company had been a dream come true, but that dream unfortunately came with all the responsibilities as well as the perks.

His thoughts turned to Meg. Since Dennis and Crista were having dinner together, that meant Meg would probably be in her hotel suite. He couldn't be in much more trouble with her than he already was, so he might as well stop by her hotel. He turned off his office light and left the building. He didn't like the feeling of always being on the defensive, an area where he didn't have much experience. But Meg could not be considered just another woman.

He had really screwed up bad when he walked out on her. For ten years, it had been eating away at his gut. Winning her back would be difficult at best, but he dedicated himself to his goal. He had steeled himself to the reality. He would do whatever he had to do no matter what it took or how long.

He drove to Meg's hotel and went straight to her room. He hesitated a moment, took a steadying breath, then knocked on the door. Surprise covered her face when she opened the door.

"May I come in? I'm not disturbing anything, am I?" He desperately wanted to pull her into his arms and hold her but resisted the temptation.

She stepped aside without saying anything and motioned for him to come inside.

He gestured toward the desk where she had obviously been working. "How's it coming?"

"It's coming along fine. Dennis says he's very pleased with the pictures and didn't have very many suggestions for the draft copy I showed him this afternoon. I was just working on a rewrite." She indicated the bar. "Could I offer you a drink?"

"No, nothing for me."

Meg had been wrestling with her guilty feeling over her attitude with Blaine that afternoon. She had been out of line when she snapped at him because of what he said. She had overreacted. Pretty soon he'd be afraid to say anything for fear of upsetting her. But first, something else had happened that she needed to bring to his attention.

"Blaine?"

He noted her slightly confused expression. "Yes?"

"I had this message on voice mail when I got in this evening. I copied it down." She handed him the note where she had copied down the message. "What does this mean?"

Blaine scanned the message, then slowly read it

again taking in every word. *Miss Wainwright, Please be good enough to ring me first thing Monday to discuss a business proposition I believe you will find financially rewarding.*

The caller identified himself as Sir Geoffrey Lewiston and gave the name of his prestigious publishing house and phone number.

Blaine handed the message back to her. His hand trembled with anger, and his jaw locked in a tight clench. "It means, my darling, that a situation I thought had been handled has reared its ugly head again. Sir Geoffrey hasn't finished interfering with my business."

He pulled his cell phone from his pocket and hit a speed dial number. "Harry. I give you two words…Sir Geoffrey. That's right, he's still at it. He left a message for Meg at her hotel to call him about *a financially rewarding business proposition*. That, combined with the episode involving Emily, makes me wonder how many other people in my employ he's trying to contact. Isn't there some legal thing you can do to stop him from harassing my employees?"

Blaine listened intently to Harry's reply. "Well, Blaine, technically, Miss Wainwright isn't your employee. She's an independent contractor working on a specific assignment. Sir Geoffrey is well within his rights to contact her about future employment, but I'll look into who else he may have contacted."

"Let me know what you come up with." Blaine disconnected the call without even saying goodbye. He stood quietly for a moment longer as he took a calming breath and turned back to Meg.

"Sorry about that. Now…where were we?" He saw the troubled look on her face. "Is something wrong,

Meg?"

"Are you okay?" Concern touched her voice.

He offered her a reassuring smile. "Of course, I'm okay. However, you look like you have something on your mind. What's wrong?"

"No, nothing's wrong—exactly. Blaine...Blaine I want to apologize for my behavior this afternoon. I shouldn't have said that to you." She wrinkled her brow in a moment of concentration as if trying to gather her words.

He put his hands on her shoulders. "That's okay. You don't need to apologize. I was careless in what I was saying. I shouldn't have blurted that out without thinking."

"I guess I just overreacted. I can't take every word you say and turn it into some kind of personal statement."

He drew her against his body and held her. She offered no resistance as she put her arms around his waist and laid her head against his shoulder. He placed his fingertips beneath her chin, lifted her face, and covered her mouth with his in tender loving care.

*****

The next three days went smoothly. Crista and Dennis had lunch Thursday noon, continuing their cautious quest for a more personal level to their existing relationship and friendship. They reconfirmed their dinner plans for that Friday evening.

Meg spent a day shooting in and around Windsor, a location close to London, and finished her rewrite of the London section to Dennis' satisfaction. By Friday afternoon, she had wrapped up everything and was ready to start on the countryside first thing Monday morning.

Friday afternoon turned into evening. Meg and Blaine lay in bed. She snuggled in his arms as he languidly trailed his fingertips across her skin. He broke their silent reverie. "Come away with me for the weekend. We can go wherever you'd like. We can stay in a castle in Ireland, go up to Scotland. What do you say?"

"It's a very tempting invitation, but if I'm going to be shooting in the countryside on Monday, I need to finish my research and nail down the specifics of my itinerary. The only specifics I have right now are hotel and travel reservations along with a list of cities and suggestions of attractions. You have a really tight deadline on this book. I can't waste time because I'm not prepared and don't know where I'm going every minute."

His fingertips lightly traced circles on her bare skin.

Her breathing noticeably quickened. "Blaine, are you listening to what I'm saying?"

"Of course, I'm listening. You said you couldn't think of anything you'd rather be doing—" He stopped to nuzzle her neck and kiss her throat. "—than to be with me in a romantic weekend hideaway—" He kissed her shoulders. "—where we could make long, drawn-out passionate love—" He kissed each breast. "—all day and all night." He kissed the soft skin between her breasts. "We wouldn't need to pack any clothes because—" He kissed her tenderly on the throat as he slowly rolled her over on top of him. "—we won't be getting out of bed."

There were no more pretenses on Meg's part. She was as hopelessly in love with Blaine as she had been ten years ago. A moment of doubt tried to invade her reverie. Had she made the biggest mistake of her life? She loved him with all her heart, but did she dare trust him again? Had she already opened herself up to the same type of pain he had inflicted on her ten years ago?

And her biggest concern of all... If he ended up walking away again, would she be able to survive it a second time?

All her thoughts stopped—both the doubts and fears as well as the certainties. The torrid sensations of his touch raced through her veins, leaving her lost in wave after wave of primal desire. They simply could not get enough of each other.

****

Blaine woke when Meg turned over in his arms. He watched her for a moment as she slept. He glanced at the clock on the nightstand. Two-thirty in the morning. She had not given him an answer about going away for the weekend, but she had been right about needing to prepare for the upcoming week. He debated whether he should wake her before going home or spend the rest of the night. As much as he wanted to stay, he knew if he spent the night, he would not want to leave in the morning.

His gaze traveled along the lines of her body, then he studied her beautiful face. He simply could not bring himself to leave her bed. He carefully tightened his arms around her, pulling her closer. She stirred slightly as he gently kissed her cheek. She slowly opened her eyes and focused on him.

"What time is it?" Sleep clung to her words. "It feels like the middle of the night."

"Shh. That's because it is the middle of the night. It's two-thirty in the morning. Now, go back to sleep."

"I'm sort of awake now. Do you know what I'd like to do?"

He rolled over on his back and laughed quietly while faking a painful moan. "Meg, you're going to be the death of me. You will surely turn me into an old man before my time." He spread his arms out at his sides and looked up at the ceiling. "Okay, do with me what you want. I don't have the strength or will to resist you."

She laughed and tousled his sandy locks with her hand. "You idiot. That's not what I had in mind." She flashed a wry grin. "At least not what I had in mind at the moment."

Clutching his chest, he let out an exaggerated sigh of relief. "Oh, thank God. I'm not sure my heart could have withstood the stimulation." He rolled over to his side and propped himself up on one elbow as he looked at her. "Okay, tell me. What is it you'd like to do? What type of pleasure may I provide you?"

She tentatively reached up and lightly touched his cheek. She glanced toward the window, the sound of the rain having captured her attention. "When did it start raining?"

"About an hour ago. At least that's when I first heard the patter against the windows." A thought suddenly occurred to him. "You should be able to get the majority of your work done by the time the rain stops. We can spend the rest of the afternoon and evening together. Would you like to go out somewhere?" He nuzzled the side of her neck. "Or would you rather stay inside?"

A soft moan of delight escaped her throat. "Mmmm…I thought you were an exhausted wreck of a man who had absolutely no energy left."

"I'm willing to make the supreme sacrifice."

"I'll make things easy for you. I'd like to see the new musical at the Savoy, if you can get tickets at this late date, literally the last moment."

"Consider it done." His breathing quickened." Do you have somewhere special you'd like to have dinner?"

"No, wherever you pick will be fine. Do you want to ask Crista if she'd like to join us?"

"I'll see if she has any plans. Crista comes to London often enough that she has friends of her own here. I really don't have to entertain her when she's in town. It makes her visits very convenient for both of us. If I'm busy at work or need to be out of town, I know she won't be sitting alone at my place being bored."

The sensation of her hand on his bare thigh drove all the thoughts from his mind. All, that is, but one. He placed a tender kiss on her cheek as he wrapped her tightly in his embrace.

"I declare this conversation concluded." He captured her mouth with a torrid kiss, one that quickly escalated as the desires rampaged through his body.

Chapter Ten

Meg woke at seven that morning and found Blaine watching her, his arms still wrapped around her body. She slowly stretched, running her foot along his bare leg, her voice thick with sleep. "Have you been awake very long?"

"About fifteen minutes. I was afraid to move. I didn't want to disturb you. I slept soundly. How about you? I didn't keep you awake by doing something terrible like snoring, did I?"

"As I remember, you never used to snore. Is this some recent thing?"

He flashed a teasing grin. "I haven't had any complaints." The smile quickly faded from his face as alarm and concern moved to the forefront. He had not meant to allude to other times when he had spent the entire night with other women. He watched her face for any sign of anger or hurt. To his relief, her features remained blissfully content. Maybe she hadn't heard him.

"If you're wondering whether or not I heard that, I did." It was as if she had read his mind. "I simply can't imagine anyone who spent the night with you having any complaints."

Her forthright statement caught him by surprise. Could it be that their awkward period of readjustment had finally been resolved? A sense of euphoria soared inside him. He pulled her tighter against his body and buried his face in her long golden hair. So many things he wanted to say to her. So many things he *needed* to say, but he couldn't seem to manage any of the right words.

They remained wrapped in each other's arms, enjoying the nearness and warmth.

Finally Meg stirred. "This is delightful, but we've got to get up. If I'm going to complete my work today, I need to get started." She wiggled out of his arms, then slid out of bed. "Shall I order us something from room service?"

"No, I'd better get my clothes on and see if I can slip out of here without attracting the attention of the entire hotel staff." He grasped her hand. "Are you sure you have to get this work done? What kind of a slave driver are you working for?"

She smiled and kissed him on the cheek. "He's a terrible task master, but the fringe benefits are great." She gave him a teasing pat on his bare bottom as he reached for his clothes.

"I can't talk you into taking the day off?"

"You know as well as I do that I have to get this finished before Monday."

"Yes, you're right. I'll be going. I'll give you a call about three or so to see how you're doing. That was the new musical at the Savoy?"

"Right."

He leaned over and kissed her softly on the lips. "I'll see you later."

He walked out of the bedroom, through the parlor room, and out the door. After retrieving his car, he drove straight home, arriving just as the clock chimed eight.

Crista sat in front of the large picture windows,

drinking coffee and reading the morning paper. She looked up in mock surprise. "Why Blaine, eight o'clock in the morning. My, my, my…that really was a late night at the office, wasn't it? You must surely be all caught up with your work by now."

He picked up a decorative pillow from the couch and playfully threw it at her. "You're impossible, you know that? And, Ms. Guardian of the Nation's Morals, what time did you and Dennis finally part company last night? Or should I say this morning?"

"Got you there. I was home by nine o'clock, and Dennis was gone five minutes later. Surprised?"

He wrinkled his brow in concern. "Yes, I am. That's a very early evening for Dennis. Did something go wrong?"

"No, not at all. In fact, he's due here at ten this morning to pick me up. We're going to drive out into the countryside for lunch." She turned her attention out the window to the rain falling on the Thames. "Of course, we made these plans before it started raining."

"Don't worry. Dennis is like the U.S. Postal Service. *Neither snow nor rain nor heat nor gloom of night stays these couriers from the swift completion of their appointed rounds.* Is there any more of that coffee? I could use a cup."

He disappeared into the kitchen and returned with a large mug of hot coffee, then continued on to his bedroom. Fifteen minutes later, he reappeared, having taken a shower and dressed in faded old jeans. After refilling his coffee mug, he sat down and thoughtfully sipped his coffee as he watched the rain.

Crista broke the silence. "Dare I ask where you've been and what you've been doing all night long?"

He gave her a sidelong look and did not make any effort to answer her question.

"Never mind. Let me rephrase that. How are things going with Meg?"

He rose and headed to the kitchen to get more coffee, pausing at the kitchen door long enough to shoot her a quick look and a teasing grin. "Terrific."

As he poured himself some more coffee, the phone rang.

Crista called out to Blaine as she reached for the phone. "I'll get it."

Dennis' voice sounded slightly harried from the other end of the phone line. "I'm running a little late. I'll be there about ten-fifteen if that's okay with you."

She looked out the window. "It's raining. Do you still want to drive out into the countryside for lunch?"

"We can't let a little rain ruin our day, unless you'd rather not. Besides, just because it's raining here doesn't mean it's raining elsewhere."

"Hey, you only go around once." There was a long silence, and she began to wonder if he was still on the line. "Dennis? Are you still there?"

"Crista…Crista, I was awake very late last night thinking about you…about us, and I was wondering…"

She waited for him to finish his sentence, but he didn't say anything else. "Yes? You were wondering what?"

"Well…never mind, luv. I'll see you shortly."

"Sure, Dennis. See you then. Bye."

Blaine came out of the kitchen. "Who was that?"

"Oh, it was only Dennis. He's running a little late."

"It looks like I'll miss him. I have a ton of errands to take care of this morning, including trying to dig up

some good seats for tonight's performance at the Savoy."
He looked at his watch. "In fact, if I'm not out of here by
nine-thirty, I won't get everything done in time."

He took another drink of his coffee and grabbed the
front section of the newspaper. He glanced at it, then
looked back at Crista. "Would you like to join us for
dinner and the theater, or is lunch with Dennis going to
take all day and all night?"

She shot him a sharp look. "Sarcasm doesn't
become you, Blaine."

He scrunched up his face and shrugged his shoulders
in a half-hearted apology. "The invitation is sincere. In
fact, it was Meg's suggestion."

"Tell Meg I appreciate her thinking of me, but I
doubt I'll be back before you leave for the evening." She
paused, her thoughts changing to ones of cautious
curiosity. "How well do you really know Dennis?"

"What do you mean by *how well*?"

"For instance, I know there's no way you can be
paying him the amount of money he needs to support his
lifestyle. His clothes are very expensive. Not just
expensive off-the-rack, they're custom tailored
expensive. Each year, he has a new car. His dating habits
alone would be enough to bankrupt the normal person.
He's always at the most expensive restaurants and
private clubs, and there's the top-of-the-line theater
tickets. I don't know where he lives, but if it fits in with
the rest of his lifestyle, it must be someplace pretty
expensive. Even if he lives in a one room dump to save
money, his obvious expenses are huge. How does he
afford it?"

Blaine contemplated her question and tried to
formulate an answer. "I'm not sure anybody really

knows Dennis that well. At least not the person inside. He first came to work for me a little over eight years ago. I was struggling, trying to get Pendragon off the ground and was in desperate need of a top-notch editor. Dennis was well known throughout the industry as an excellent editor. He had started working in the publishing business fourteen years earlier, fresh out of college.

"One afternoon, he just wandered into my office and said he heard I was looking for someone. We talked for a while, then I said I would like him to come to work for me, but there was no way I could afford to pay him what he was currently earning, let alone an increase. He looked me square in the eye and asked what I could afford to pay. I gave him the number in my budget, fully prepared for him to laugh in my face then walk out. But instead, without hesitation, he said he'd take it.

"My mouth fell open. It must have been a full minute before I could get it together to say anything. I asked him why he was willing to work for me at considerably less money than he had been making, especially when his services were widely in demand.

"He said he liked what I was trying to accomplish and the way I was going about it. He told me he had just come into an inheritance so money wasn't a consideration. He liked the type of work he did and intended to continue even though he no longer needed to work."

Crista's face brightened. "An inheritance? That certainly explains a lot."

"He went to work for me the next day. He took a chance on me, and I can honestly say he's been a big factor in my success. He's never asked for more money. I've given him salary increases, of course, but he's never asked. He never abuses his expense account. In fact, I'm aware of legitimate expenses over the years that he's never turned in. I have the best managing editor in the business for a lot less than the salary he could command from one of the major publishing houses. I really owe Dennis a lot."

Confusion and pain darted through him. "That's probably why I'm having such a difficult time dealing with this situation between him and Meg. If it was anyone else, I'd fire him without giving it a second thought." He sat in silence for a moment, lost in his thoughts, then rose and wandered back to the kitchen. He came out in a few minutes eating a toasted muffin. "I'd better get moving before it gets any later." He continued on to his bedroom and returned hopping on one foot while trying to slip his shoe on the other foot. "Well, have a good lunch. I'll see you later." He gave Crista a kiss on the cheek, then headed for the door.

The ringing phone interrupted as Crista cleared the morning coffee dishes. Harry was trying to locate Blaine. "He's not here right now. He's out running errands. May I take a message?"

"I'll try to reach him on his mobile phone. In case I miss him, tell him to call me right away. It's about the problems with Sir Geoffrey. Tell Blaine he's at it again. I'll be at home all day."

"I'll leave the message for him." She placed the written message on the bar where he would find it, then went into her bedroom to put on her makeup and get dressed.

She studied the clothes hanging in her closet. The weather presented her with a problem. With the rain and the fact that they would be riding in the car for a while, she needed to dress comfortably and warmly. She selected a pair of slacks and a sweater along with low-heeled comfortable shoes. After she dressed, she checked her appearance in the full-length mirror. She nodded her head in approval. All the aerobics had really paid off.

Dennis arrived promptly at ten-fifteen. He gave her an appreciative look as he entered the living room. "As usual, luv, you look smashing."

"Thanks. Now, tell me, what was all that stammering on the phone?"

He took both of her hands in his and looked at her for a long moment. "I spent a lot of time last night thinking about you...about us. Do you suppose...I mean, would you..."

"Dennis, what's wrong with you? If you have something to say, just spit it out."

"Okay, here goes." He took a steadying breath and started talking. "Crista, would you pack a bag and come away with me for the weekend? We could stay at a charming country inn, sit in front of the fireplace, sip champagne, and watch the rain falling outside the windows. We could dine at a quiet, romantic restaurant and spend the rest of the night making passionate love."

He seemed to be holding his breath, waiting for her response with a considerable amount of trepidation covering his face. She looked into his searching eyes, saw his anxiety and uncertainty. She squeezed his hands and smiled at him. "Yes, I would like that very much."

He broke out in a big smile. "Yes? Just like that?"

She chuckled softly at his almost boyish excitement and enthusiasm. "Yes. Just like that."

He wrapped his arms around her, holding her in his

embrace for a minute before pulling back so he could see her. "Are you sure you want to do this?"

She tilted her head, raised a questioning eyebrow, and shot him a quizzical look. "Are you trying to back out."

"No way."

Her amused smile turned into a laugh. "You sound like you've never had a woman agree to spend the night with you before, and we both know that's not so."

"You're not just any woman. You're someone very special." He lowered his mouth to hers and bestowed a kiss that started out tender and gentle but soon conveyed a sense of urgency and sensual earthiness.

She responded with a smoldering passion that caught Dennis totally off guard. His voice took on a slight huskiness that surprised him. "This is a side of you I didn't expect." He lowered his mouth to hers again, his tongue teasing as it darted between her lips.

Her breathing grew more rapid. "If we don't stop doing this, I won't be able to pack that bag so we can get out of here."

He drew back and looked into her eyes. Her intense sexuality reached out and grabbed him. "If you don't stop looking at me like that, I won't be able to stop doing this." He recaptured her mouth as he pulled her body tightly against his. She wrapped her arms around him, massaging the back of his neck and running her fingers through his hair.

"Whew…tell me, luv, is it unbearably hot in here, or is it just my imagination? I feel like I'm being consumed by flames." He looked at her. "Flames of passion."

He reached for her mouth again, but she pulled back.

"Let me pack that bag so we can leave."

Begrudgingly, he released her from his arms. "Okay, but hurry."

"I'll only be a minute."

He watched as she went to her bedroom, then he wandered slowly around the living room and over to the bar. The note Crista had left for Blaine caught his eye. He picked it up, glanced back toward her closed bedroom door, then read the message. A swift surge of anger darted through him as he replaced the note on the bar. He stood for a moment lost in thought, then reached into his inside jacket pocket and withdrew his phone. He entered a quick notation.

He continued wandering aimlessly around the living room. His gaze finally settled on the portrait of Meg. He sat and stared at it, taking in every detail, every brush stroke. He became totally absorbed in the emotions the painting pulled out of him. Emotions as confusing and uncomfortable as they were profound.

When Crista came back into the room carrying her overnight bag, she saw him staring intently at the painting. She watched him for a moment. "What is it you find so fascinating about that painting? Is it the subject matter or the artwork?"

He turned to her and offered a somewhat distracted smile before returning his attention to the painting. "I don't know. It's something I can't explain. It's more of a feeling I get from it." He stared at the painting a moment longer before turning toward Crista. "Does she love him as much as he obviously loves her?"

Crista sensed a sadness about him, an emptiness of some sort. "I don't know, and neither does Blaine." Then she added softly, "I believe she did at one time, but that was a long time ago. I don't know about now."

She continued to watch Dennis as he stared at the painting for a moment longer. Then he turned toward her and snapped back to the familiar Dennis she had always known. She realized at that moment just how lonely he must really be, how his happy-go-lucky lifestyle was a total façade, something he hid behind so no one could get too close to him. How much he longed for that special someone to share his life.

He flashed his sexy smile and gave her a wink. "Well, luv, shall we go?"

The rain continued to gently cover the countryside as they drove west out of London toward the Cotswolds. Their conversation remained casual and light, although the anxiety he obviously felt concerning the change in their relationship showed on his face. He looked more like a schoolboy nervously going on his first date.

He wasn't the only one feeling the anxiety. Apprehension filled Crista's thoughts. She wondered if, after twenty-five years of faithful marriage, she could take this sudden leap into the world of sexual liberation. She consciously wanted this but didn't feel as emotionally prepared for it as she wanted to be—or as she thought she was.

She had often kidded with Dennis over the years about this eventuality. *"If I wasn't married…"* But she never believed that situation would be a reality, that she would ever be a divorced woman.

Crista looked at him, studied his handsome profile, felt the pull of his magnetic sex appeal. A nervous tremor moved through her body as her fears and insecurities came to the surface. He had spent his adult life pursuing and bedding truly stunning women. Hopefully, he wouldn't find her too much of a disappointment.

He gave her one of his best sexy smiles and a wink. "You look like the proverbial lamb who's being led to the slaughter. Are you having second thoughts? If you want to change your mind, it's not too late."

She mustered up a reassuring smile. "Now, why would I want to change my mind? Look how long it took me to talk you into this. You've been playing hard to get for the entire eight years I've known you."

He laughed an open, easy laugh. "You mean I was the one who kept us from doing this?" He reached over and put his hand over hers, his voice gentle and reassuring. "Don't be nervous, Crista. Nothing will happen this weekend unless you want it to."

They drove along for a little while in silence, then he pulled the car over to the side of the road. He took her face in his hands and placed a tender kiss on her lips. "I can understand your anxiety. In fact, I share your anxiety. Being here with you... This is something new for me, too."

She offered him a shy smile. "Thanks. I guess I talk a better game than I play."

"We can turn around and go back right now if you wish." His hesitant voice conveyed a hint of his anxiety over the turn of events. "Would you like to go back to London?"

She squeezed his hand and smiled. "No, I don't want to go back to London. I want the weekend you promised me. All of it."

He returned her smile, not his sexy come-on smile, but a sincere one. "We'll have a nice weekend, honest we will. And remember, we can go back to London any time you say."

She leaned over and kissed him on the cheek. He pulled the car back on the road as he put his arm around her and drew her to his side.

They drove up in front of the country inn. "Wait here where it's dry. I'll be right back." He dashed through the rain to the entrance and went to the registration desk. She could see Dennis talking intently with the clerk, then slipping him some cash as the clerk smiled and handed over a registration card.

Dennis hurried back to the car and opened the door on the passenger side. "I had a little difficulty talking the clerk into giving us a room with a fireplace, but he finally saw the error of his ways." He held out his hand to help her from the car. "I hope you like the room."

He carried their overnight bags as they walked down the hall. He opened the door then stepped aside so she could enter the room. She turned to him, her eyes wide with surprise and pleasure, her face aglow with delight. The bright, cheery room had a king-size bed with a brass headboard and a bedspread that matched the drapes. Large windows provided a view of the lush green countryside and rolling hills. A comfortable couch had been placed in front of the wood burning fireplace on the other side of the tastefully decorated room.

"It's a beautiful room." She walked over to the windows and looked out, her figure silhouetted against the rain streaked glass.

He watched her with a smoldering intensity. His eyes devoured her, his voice soft and serious. "Crista, you're very beautiful. Have I ever told you that before?"

"No, not in those exact words." Her voice softened as the emotion flowed through her. "And not with that much sincerity in your voice."

"Well, you are." He held her gaze for a long moment, then crossed the room. "Let's go have lunch. I'll build a fire when we get back."

Three hours later, Dennis and Crista burst through the door of their room convulsed in spasms of laughter, enjoying the silly mood created by the adventure in the rain. She shook the water from her umbrella, then placed it in the umbrella stand. "I can't believe the way it's coming down out there. And you…changing that flat tire in the rain."

She started to laugh again at the sight of the always impeccably groomed Dennis Mallory splattered with mud and dripping water on the floor. He laughed as he grabbed her and pulled her against his chest. "I never realized, luv, what a vicious sense of humor you have. Brand new expensive cars are not supposed to get flat tires."

They held each other's gazes for a long, intense moment.

"Here, let me help you with that damp jacket. I don't want you to catch a chill. I'll get a fire started straight away." He helped her out of her jacket, then went immediately to the fireplace. A few minutes later, he had a crackling blaze warming the room.

"Now, luv, you sit here by the fire while I—" He surveyed his own muddy clothes. "—take a quick shower and change into something that might not be fashionable, but at least, it will be clean and dry."

Crista sat in front of the fireplace, watching the flames and basking in the glow of the carefree lunch adventure. Her life had been in such turmoil for the last few months and unsettled for a year prior to that. She needed this weekend getaway.

Dennis emerged from the bathroom dressed in a pair of jeans and a long-sleeved pullover shirt, his hair tousled from the towel drying. "I may not be fashionable, but I sure feel better."

"Well, I'm surprised. I didn't think you owned something as mundane as jeans."

His eyes twinkled with good humor. "In spite of how long we've known each other, I'll bet there's lots of things about me you don't know. Maybe I can provide you with a few more surprises before the weekend is through." He opened the champagne he had arranged to have delivered to the room while they were at lunch, poured two glasses, and handed one to her. He raised his glass in a toast. "Here's to a marvelous weekend with a very special lady."

She smiled shyly, the heat of embarrassment spreading across her cheeks. "Thank you." They sipped their champagne as they looked into each other's eyes. She nervously toyed with her glass, twirling the stem between her fingers and thumb. This weekend was, indeed, what she needed. However, that intellectual thought didn't alleviate her apprehension. "Now what?"

"Why don't we just sit here in front of the fire and enjoy our champagne." His voice was soft and soothing. "Don't be nervous, Crista. Whatever happens here this weekend will happen naturally because we both want it to happen. Not because it's what you think is supposed to happen. It won't be because it's what I want. It will be because you want it to happen and no other reason." He squeezed her hand reassuringly and gave her a kiss on the cheek.

She hesitantly took another sip of her champagne. "Dennis…"

"Yes, luv?"

"Dennis…"

"What was that you so recently said to me, luv? If you have something to say, just spit it out." He raised a questioning eyebrow. "Well?"

An amused smile tugged at the corners of her mouth. "You're right, that's exactly what I said. Well, here goes." She paused for a moment to collect her thoughts. "I'm very nervous about this, about being here with you." She looked into his eyes, holding his gaze for several seconds. "The truth is I haven't made love with anyone in twenty-five years except Jack, and that finally became mechanical, then stopped altogether. I'm not sure I would know how to respond to someone new."

He put his arm reassuringly around her shoulder. She looked into his eyes again. "I need this, Dennis. My self-esteem has taken quite a beating this last year."

"Don't ever sell yourself short. You are, without a doubt, the most together woman I have ever known. You're intelligent, charming, fun, honest, beautiful…" His gaze dropped to her slightly parted lips. "And very, *very* desirable." He slowly drew her to him as he covered her mouth with his.

Sensual stirrings raced through her body as she returned his kiss. He held her tighter as their kiss became more ardent. She gently ran her fingers through his dark hair while slowly rubbing her other hand across the back of his shirt.

They remained wrapped in each other's arms as each tenderly caressed the other's face, arms, neck, and shoulders. Kissing, sometimes playfully and sometimes seriously. Enjoying the tender moments—the sensations of touch, smell, and taste. They leisurely sipped their champagne while sitting in front of the fire, watching and listening to the gentle patter of the rain against the windows. They were comfortable and content in their exploration of each other's needs and wants, in their intimate search for true feelings and emotions.

In their quest to know each other on a more personal and intimate level.

The afternoon passed into evening as the light of day faded and the rain began to let up. They had finished their bottle of champagne. He gently stroked her cheek and hair as he looked lovingly into her eyes. "Would you like to go out to dinner? I promised you a quiet meal in a romantic restaurant. There's a good place just half a mile from here."

She reached her mouth to his and kissed him lightly on the lips. "If you'll give me a minute to freshen my makeup, I'll be ready."

He rose and held out his hand to help her from the couch. "I'll call and reserve a quiet corner table, assuming you don't mind the way I'm dressed." He glanced down at his jeans. "And assuming the restaurant is okay with my attire."

She smiled warmly. "I can't speak for the restaurant, but I don't mind at all."

They shared a candlelit dinner, seemingly mesmerized by each other's presence. They sipped an after-dinner drink, their eyes locked together in a scorching intensity. Eventually, they returned to the inn and to their room where he immediately added more wood to the fire to revive the dying embers.

Dennis wrapped her in his embrace, consuming her mouth as she put her arms around his neck and returned his passion. The firelight cast shadows of their clinging bodies on the wall. Their breathing came in ragged gasps as a heightened sense of need enveloped them.

They moved in unison toward the bed as he slowly removed her sweater from her trembling body. Her shaking fingers tentatively fumbled with his shirt.

He abruptly released her sweater and captured her hands in his, steadying them as he drew her fingers away from his shirt. He raised her chin until he could look into her eyes.

"You're scared to death, aren't you?"

Crista gave him a weak smile. "It's that obvious?" She sat on the edge of the bed with Dennis sitting next to her. "Apparently the moment of truth is at hand." A nervous anxiety jittered inside her. She took a calming breath in an attempt to settle her rattled nerves, but it didn't help.

"As a friend I find you very comfortable to be with, I always have. But as a lover? The truth is, you intimidate me."

Dennis burst into a spontaneous laugh, leaving Crista stunned and hurt. He quickly gathered her in his arms and pulled her to him, still chuckling to himself. "I'm sorry, Crista. I'm not laughing at you. I'm laughing at how ludicrous that is." He pulled back just enough to be able to look into her eyes. "You say I intimidate you? Why? Because of my reputation? All the women I'm reputed to have slept with?"

She glanced away and shyly nodded. He again drew her to him, stroking her soft hair. "That's really rich, luv. The truth is most of the women I go out with couldn't carry on an intelligent conversation if their lives depended on it. We have only one thing in common and that's a healthy sex drive. We know exactly what we want from each other, no more and no less. It's all very shallow."

His voice softened as he ran his fingers through her hair. "And not very satisfying. Oh, the sex is terrific, but it's momentary and nothing else. It has no meaning attached to it, nothing personal. Nothing more than a biological function. That's probably one of the reasons I like my work so much. It provides me with a creative and intellectual outlet, keeps the old mind from stagnating and turning to pudding. My work gives me great satisfaction."

His honesty and sincerity came through in his voice. "But you are an incredibly complete package. You say I intimidate you?" He rested his cheek against the top of her head. "You, my delectable Crista, scare the hell out of me."

The tension drained from her body. She burst into laughter. "I feel so silly."

"I know what other women want from me. It's a very simple formula and always the same. It starts with dinner usually followed by dancing in a noisy club with loud music or the theater, someplace where we won't have to attempt to carry on any awkward conversation, then to bed. Sometimes, we skip step two and go straight from dinner to bed." He ran his fingers lightly across her cheek. "You, luv, are a total mystery. I'm afraid I'll be lacking, that I won't be able to provide you with what you want or need."

He looked deeply into her intense blue eyes and brushed his fingers lightly across her cheek. "What do you want, Crista? What are you hoping this weekend will be?"

Chapter Eleven

Crista looked into Dennis' questioning eyes. A little tremor of apprehension rippled through her body. She spoke hesitantly at first then with more confidence. "I want you to make love to me. Make me feel special. Make me forget the pain of the last year. Spirit me away to a place where time has no meaning. Where there aren't any rules. Where there's only joy and happiness without pressure, stress, or disappointment. Where anger and emotional turmoil don't exist."

"I'll do my best, luv." He looked longingly at her. His voice trailed off to a mere whisper. "I'll do my very best."

Slowly and sensually, they removed each other's clothing as they became enveloped in a blanket of smoldering desire. He swept her into his arms again, pressing her tightly against his body. They sank into the softness of the bed, still in each other's arms. He stroked his fingertips across her skin as he covered her neck and shoulders with soft kisses.

She found herself automatically responding to his touch, reveling in the sensations he created in her. Her skin tingled. Waves of desire swept through her body. It had been much too long since she experienced this type of excitement, so much hot unchecked passion.

So very much alive.

****

Dennis raised up on one elbow. With his other hand he tenderly smoothed several loose tendrils of hair away from her face. Then he kissed her softly on the lips. "Are you okay, Crista?"

"Mmmm…I feel like a new woman. I haven't felt this alive in more years than I care to remember."

He nuzzled her neck as his manner turned serious. "All the women I've had sex with… That's all it was, just recreational sex. It never included any kind of emotional involvement. I never realized it could be this fantastic." He looked deeply into her eyes. "You were right when you said good relationships start first as friends. I've never had that aspect before."

Crista studied him as she lightly brushed her fingers across his cheek and through his hair. She carefully chose her words as she opened what she knew would be a troublesome subject.

"Dennis, there's something we need to talk about."

"And what would that be?" He placed a series of kisses on her neck and across her shoulder.

"I'm serious." She responded to his tantalizing ministrations with a soft moan before gently shoving his hand away. "I'm serious. It's…it's about you and Meg. Blaine says you slept with her. Did you?"

He looked searchingly into her eyes. She saw the uneasiness, the many thoughts and emotions darting through him. He finally answered her. "No, I didn't."

"Blaine's firmly convinced that you did."

He again seemed to be searching her face as if seeking some sort of clue, an indication of what to do. He rolled over onto his back, taking her with him in his embrace. "I told him nothing happened between Meg and me.

"I'll tell you what happened that night. I arrived at her hotel to pick her up for dinner. I could see she was distraught, but I didn't know why. She just sort of folded into me, seeking some sort of comfort."

Crista directed a sharp look at him. "If you're going to tell it, do it honestly or don't bother. You saw an emotionally vulnerable woman and jumped all over the possibilities."

A bittersweet grin tugged at the corners of his mouth. "You know me too well, probably better than I know myself. Okay, I saw the timing was right."

A look of sadness and despair crossed his face. He put one arm behind his head as he stared up at the ceiling. Slowly, carefully measuring his words, he told her everything that happened that night, just as it happened, leaving nothing out, the expression on his face changing to one of pure anguish.

With a feeling of almost complete despair, Dennis turned back toward Crista. "I've never tried to force myself on a woman in my entire life." His voice quieted. "She slapped me and told me to get out. When I saw the terror on her face and in her eyes—" He shook his head, his voice dropping to a mere whisper. "I couldn't believe what I had done.

"It was horrible. I didn't think I was capable of that type of reprehensible behavior." He closed his eyes. "I swore to myself that I'd never repeat that sordid tale to anyone, never tell how I had behaved so shamefully toward a woman. And on top of that, a woman I truly respect. My transgression was especially appalling because I knew there was some kind of a connection between her and Blaine, even though I didn't know what it was. Without a doubt, that was the lowest, darkest moment of my life. I wanted to call her the next morning and apologize, but I simply didn't know what to say to explain or excuse my deplorable actions. I did apologize the next time I saw her. We shook hands and agreed to put it behind us, but there's no way I'll ever be able to truly put it behind me. It's something I'll never forget, something I should never forget. Something I don't deserve to have erased from my memory."

Crista had no doubts his confession had been a very difficult one, that he had been totally truthful with her. "In spite of what you said to Blaine, he still believes you and Meg made love that night. It's tearing him up inside. He's in a dilemma between his anger at you and his regard for your friendship and working relationship. You don't have to tell him the whole story if you don't want to but tell him again that you and Meg never made love. Tell him in a way so he'll believe it." She rolled over on her side and put her arm across his body. "Please, Dennis? Would you do that? For me?"

He pulled Crista over on top of him. "I'd walk barefoot on hot coals to the ends of the earth if you wanted me to."

They were lost, once again, to the incendiary waves of passion that flowed between them until they fell asleep in each other's arms.

The next morning, Crista stirred and slowly opened her eyes. The rain clouds had disappeared leaving the colors of a beautiful sunrise exposed as they streaked across the clear early morning sky. Dennis was stretched out next to her, their bodies touching. As she moved, he put his arms around her.

"Well, you're finally awake. I've been awake for about half an hour now." A mischievous grin tugged at the corners of his mouth as he began to tease her. "Yours is certainly a body I could gladly spend a lifetime getting to know, but you'll have to pardon my curiosity. Just who are you? The last thing I remember was standing at the bar talking to a group of people. Were you one of them?"

Crista noted the twinkle in his eyes and the sly smile. "Well, sir. That's not very flattering. I expect the men I spend the night with to at least remember the color of my eyes the next morning."

The twinkle quickly disappeared to be replaced by a deep caring as he gazed at her. "And the dimples on both cheeks of your bottom, your perfect breasts, the little birth mark on the inside of your upper left thigh, an addictive taste more powerful than any narcotic, and the heated passion that left me both breathless and excited."

She stared at him with total surprise. "You are observant, aren't you?"

"You're a pleasure to observe. It's an interesting family resemblance, those dimples. Of course, Blaine's are on his face while yours—" He seductively ran his hand across her bare bottom. "—have slipped a little farther down. Blaine gets more mileage out of his, but yours are much cuter." He pulled her to him, softly nuzzled her neck, and held her tightly. "Crista…I could spend the entire day right here, just like this, and never move. I've never been with anyone as totally comfortable to be with as you." He continued to hold her for a few moments longer, then his manner turned upbeat. "However, I'm hungry."

Dennis and Crista dressed and went to breakfast. He clasped her hand tightly as they walked toward the dining room, both totally enamored of each other and oblivious to their surroundings.

Dennis finally spoke. "What time would you like to start back to the city? As for me, all I have to do is be at the office on time tomorrow morning. We could stay here another night if we left very early in the morning."

Crista squeezed his hand as they continued to walk down the hallway. "Why don't we start back early this afternoon, at check-out time. That will give us the room for the rest of the morning."

He gave her a look of mild surprise as his sexy smile slowly spread across his face. "Well, well. Tell me, luv, did you have anything special in mind?"

"I thought we might just let nature take its course. Is that okay with you?"

His expression became very serious. "I can't begin to tell you how okay that is with me." He flashed his sexy smile again.

They reached the dining room and were seated for breakfast. After eating, they returned to their room and again snuggled in bed together. The sensations of his sensual touch swept through her body. Dennis made sure she was satisfied before taking anything for himself. Her husband had never made her feel so special, had never unselfishly catered to what pleased her. All thoughts faded as the intense ecstasy of his touch wholly consumed her.

Dennis and Crista remained ensconced in bed until check out time. They quickly packed and prepared to leave. As he opened the door for her, she turned back and took one last look at the room. He put his arm protectively around her shoulders and kissed her on the cheek. His words were soft, his voice filled with honesty.

"When we left London I had no idea what would

happen this weekend. I can honestly say I felt a great deal of apprehension and anxiety. I've always felt very close to you. I didn't know how this change in our relationship would turn out." He put both hands on her shoulders and turned her to face him. "I don't know when I've enjoyed a weekend more." He paused while looking into her eyes. "Crista, you're going to have to help me out here. Dealing honestly with emotions and feelings is not what I do best."

She laughed. "I know. It's an area where you have virtually no experience."

He pulled her to him. "Come on now, give me a break. I'm trying to say something very serious, something from inside me, and I don't know how to go about it." He continued to hold her for a moment longer, then pulled back to look into her eyes again. "You're very special to me. This weekend has been very special to me. I want to spend much more time with you."

He rested his cheek against her head. "I'm sorry for the pain you're feeling because of your divorce." He placed a tender kiss on her forehead. "But as for me, I couldn't be more thrilled about the breakup of a marriage. Now that I've found you, really found you, I don't want to lose you." He lowered his face to hers, placing a gentle kiss on her lips.

She put her arms around his neck and returned his kiss, not passionately but tenderly and with feeling. "That's the nicest thing anyone has ever said to me. This weekend was very important to me, too. You've made me feel very special. It's been a long time since I've felt so alive." They both took one last look at the room, then drove back to London.

Dennis pulled his car up to the curb in front of

Blaine's apartment. He carried Crista's bag as they slowly walked to the door, his other arm around her shoulders. He leaned forward and kissed her. "Will you have dinner with me tomorrow night?"

"Yes, I'd love to."

"Good. I have a busy day. Would you mind meeting me at the office, say about six o'clock?"

"No, I wouldn't mind at all. I'll see you then."

He again kissed her. She went inside.

Crista set her overnight bag by her bedroom door and walked across the room to the large windows overlooking the Thames River. She stood there watching the river flowing and the cars crossing Tower Bridge. A slight smile turned the corners of her lips as she thought back over the weekend. She had never felt as desirable as she had for the past two days, and she had Dennis to thank for it.

She had enjoyed a side of Dennis she never dreamed existed, the person hidden behind the happy-go-lucky façade he presented to everyone. But what kind of relationship did they now have? What would their future be? She had already invested twenty-five years in a marriage and had two grown children. Was she really ready to jump from one relationship directly into another one? She cared about Dennis very much, very much indeed.

Then another thought hit her. She had been pondering where their relationship was going, but did they really have a *relationship*? Something of a romantic nature rather than close friends? What had the weekend meant to Dennis? Was she projecting something that existed only in her mind? Were they now simply friends with benefits? She needed to keep what had happened in a logical perspective.

Crista remained lost in her thoughts as she continued to stare out at the river.

"Well, you and Dennis must have had quite a lunch."

She turned at the sound of Blaine's voice, a voice cloaked in sarcasm, and saw him framed in his bedroom door. She shot him a hard look. "I had a marvelous weekend." A sharp edge clung to her words, almost like a warning. "Don't spoil it for me."

"Sorry. Okay, tell me about it—but only the G-rated parts."

"There's a side of Dennis you've never seen…a caring, vulnerable, and sometimes even uncertain person."

"Dennis? Come on, you don't really expect me to buy that, do you? I've never known anyone more sure of himself than Dennis. That's sure of himself without it translating into arrogance. Dennis is not arrogant. I'll give him that."

"Yes, I do expect you to believe it. I had a great time this weekend. I was feeling uncertain about my own worth. You know, being married to the same man for twenty-five years then suddenly finding yourself adrift, discovering that you're someone alone and no longer part of a couple even though we hadn't been an emotionally connected couple for quite a while… Well, it's pretty scary. You begin to doubt your ability to compete in the world as your own person, to be desirable, and to be able to respond rather than merely react. Dennis and I talked a great deal during the weekend, talked sincerely and openly about so many different things. He was caring, tender, supportive, and honest. He made me feel special. He provided a real boost to my self-esteem. He restored my sense of self-worth."

Blaine's manner turned serious. "I know you've had a pretty rough time of it for the last year, and I haven't been very supportive. I even compounded it by involving you in my problems when you already had enough problems of your own. I'm sorry, Crista. What can I do to help?"

She smiled as she put her arms around him and gave him a hug. "Just be there if I need you."

"I should have been there for you this weekend instead of leaving you in a position where you had to turn to Dennis for comfort and support."

"I didn't have to turn to Dennis, I *chose* to turn to Dennis. After all"—she gave him a wink and wry smile as she withdrew her embrace—"Dennis was able to provide certain comforts that society would frown on coming from my brother."

"Crista!" Blaine's irritation immediately flared. "Why do you say things like that?"

"Because they shock you, my darling brother. You want your pleasures but occasionally become a little self-righteous when other people want theirs."

"Are we talking about Dennis again?"

"Yes, we are. He opened up and shared his own fears and concerns about his life and his future. You know, Dennis is not the happy-go-lucky person that he would have you and everyone else believe. A lot of that extremely smooth exterior is only a façade for him to hide behind. Maybe something will come of this and maybe not, but I can tell you one thing. I will always be very close to him, and I think he feels the same."

Crista eyed Blaine carefully. "I can tell you

something else, too, that will probably surprise you. He considers you his best friend. He has the highest regard and respect for you, Blaine."

"Dennis said that? About me?"

"Yes. He said that, and I believe he meant it, too."

Blaine shook his head in disbelief as he turned to walk back to his bedroom, mumbling to himself. "Dennis said that? About me?"

The rest of the day passed quickly for Blaine. He attended to some personal errands and took care of a little business. But the blossoming relationship between his sister and Dennis never strayed far from his thoughts.

That evening found Blaine at Meg's hotel. They ate dinner at the hotel restaurant, then went back to her suite. He carried his somber mood with him.

"Is something wrong? You seem very quiet."

"Oh, it's nothing." He pursed his lips and wrinkled his brow into a frown. "Yes, it is something. Crista and Dennis spent the weekend together, and I guess I'm having a little trouble accepting it. Their eight years as good friends suddenly turned into something physical. Then she dropped another bombshell on me. It seems Dennis considers me his best friend. He apparently has a great deal of respect for me."

She put her arms around him. "Crista is one of the most level-headed women and the best judge of character I've ever met. I'm sure she knows what she's doing."

Blaine pulled Meg into his embrace. "Yes, I'm sure you're right." They stood holding each other for a few moments, then he let go of her. "I'd better leave so you can get your stuff together and get some sleep." He looked into her eyes. "I'm going to miss you. I'll see you Thursday evening when you get back. We'll have dinner." He kissed her, then turned to leave.

"Blaine?"

He immediately noticed her pensive expression. "What's wrong? You look like something is bothering you."

"It's probably nothing. I was just thinking...contemplating the future." She paused, her voice reflecting her uncertainty. "Blaine, what's the future for us? You orchestrated this entire situation. What did you intend to have happen? Where is this headed? Where do we go from here?"

He looked at her, searching her face for some clue to her mood. "I don't know. What would you like it to be? You once asked me what I wanted from you. Well, I don't have a clue what you want from me. What do you see for the future?" He ran his fingers through her mussed hair. "I'll do whatever you want. I'll give you everything I can."

They looked at each other, neither one speaking.

Finally, he broke the silence. "Meg?"

"I don't know, Blaine." Her voice faltered as she hesitated, then she slowly shook her head as she took a step away from him. "I don't know. You've had me so confused, I don't know what to think or feel."

Silence surrounded them. The air had become tinged with a touch of sadness and doubt. She finally spoke. "I still have a little work to do before I leave for the countryside in the morning. I'd better get to it."

He put his hands on her shoulders. "I'll let you get to work."

He kissed her tenderly on the lips then left. Nothing had been resolved. The question about their future continued to hang uneasily in the air.

****

Dennis sat in his living room, a drink in hand. An odd mixture of confusion and contentment swirled around inside him. He replayed the events of the last two days through his mind. He had never spent a more enjoyable weekend with a woman. Crista represented what he had been searching for all his adult life. She encompassed everything he had ever wanted and everything he needed.

A frown wrinkled across his forehead. She also happened to be Blaine's sister.

According to Crista, Blaine was upset with him over Meg and that was before he had spent the weekend with Blaine's sister. Crista had been right about one thing. He had to tell Blaine again that he and Meg never had sex, and this time he had to make sure Blaine believed him. He also needed to get his feelings and thoughts together concerning Crista. He had never been in this type of quandary. Up until now, his life had been basically uncomplicated—work, sex, sleep, repeat.

But now...now, he wasn't sure about anything. His life had been turned upside down and inside out. What kind of relationship did he and Crista have? Or, more importantly, what kind of relationship did they want? He didn't know what Crista wanted for the future, a problem compounded by the fact that he didn't know what he wanted, either.

For a brief moment, he allowed the notion to seep into his consciousness that he might even be falling in love with her, a thought that definitely frightened him. He had never before entertained the notion of actually being in love. Or even being in a committed relationship with one woman.

Chapter Twelve

Blaine arrived at his office very early Monday to finish up some paperwork before starting his normal day. About an hour later, Dennis stuck his head around the corner. Blaine shot him a questioning look. The casual smile faded from Dennis' face to be replaced by an uncomfortable concern.

He closed the office door and walked over to Blaine's desk. "I guess you and I need to talk—or more accurately, I need to talk. About this weekend... I want you to know that I don't think of Crista as just another of my many women. She's a very special lady, and I care about her very much."

Blaine gave him a long hard look. "You seem to have inserted yourself very nicely into my personal life. First Meg and now my sister."

"That's the other thing. About your finding my necktie in Meg's suite..." Dennis shifted his weight from one foot to the other as he glanced awkwardly at the floor then up at Blaine again. "I told you nothing happened, and that's the truth, but not because I didn't try. I made a pass at her and she responded by slapping my face and telling me to leave. I spent the rest of the evening elsewhere soothing my bruised ego."

A feeling of relief settled over Blaine as a slight smile curled the corners of his mouth. "Thanks, Dennis. I know that was probably difficult for you to admit. It's not your style."

Dennis smiled and reached out his hand toward Blaine. "Are we still friends, or am I about to be unemployed?"

Blaine shook his hand and gave him a reassuring smile. "Yes, Dennis. We're still friends. However, you and Crista... That will take a little getting used to."

Dennis gave an embarrassed shrug of his shoulders. "Yes, it's something new for me, too. An entirely different type of relationship. But you know what? I like it." He straightened and turned to leave Blaine's office. "I have something urgent to attend to. See you later."

The day continued to be busy for everyone and passed quickly. As Blaine prepared to leave his office at five-thirty, Meg called to report on her progress. They talked for a little while about the assignment and the next day's shooting. "It's going to seem like forever before you're back in London on Thursday."

"I know what you mean. But for now, I'd better grab some dinner, then get myself together for tomorrow. I'll talk to you when I get back to my hotel tomorrow evening."

After they hung up, Blaine sat at his desk staring blankly at the phone.

"Hi. You look like you're trying to solve all the world's problems in one sitting."

He looked up at the sound of Crista's voice. "This is a surprise. I'm always happy to see you, but what are you doing here?"

"I'm meeting Dennis. We're going out to dinner. Why are you in such deep concentration?"

"Oh, it's Meg. I just got off the phone with her."

A look of concern flashed across Crista's face. "Is

she okay?"

"Oh, yeah. It's nothing like that." Blaine paused to gather his thoughts. "You know what? I don't know how she really feels about me. She just said she missed me, but I don't know exactly what that means. I've asked her what she wants for the future. I've told her I'd give her anything in my power to give, but I still don't know what she's thinking." He made eye contact with Crista. "I don't know if she loves me."

Crista put her hand on his shoulder and gave it a squeeze. "Maybe she just needs a little more time. I'm sure this hasn't been easy for her. Tell me, Blaine, what do you want for the future?"

"I want whatever Meg will allow me. If we continue on like this and that's all she'll allow, then I guess I'll have to accept that as the way it will be and live with it. As for me, I want Meg to marry me. I want her to be my wife. I want us to spend the rest of our lives together."

"Have you asked her to marry you?"

"No. Until I know whether or not she really loves me, there's no point in asking her." He brightened his expression. "You didn't come here to listen to me complain about my trials and tribulations. Dennis is probably in his office." He paused for a moment then continued, his voice thoughtful. "Dennis and I had a talk this morning. It was brief but interesting. He told me what he had told me before, that he and Meg never had sex. He did elaborate on what happened, that he made a pass it her and she slapped him. And you know what? I really do believe what he said. I think he was actually being straight with me."

"Good, I'd glad that's settled." She gave him a quick hug, then hurried toward Dennis' office.

Blaine turned out his office lights and went home.

****

Tuesday morning presented another busy day. The tight deadline on Meg's book had Dennis devoting full time to her copy and pictures. Blaine still wrestled with paperwork, what he referred to as *the burden of command*. The time he had taken from his schedule to spend with Meg had put him way behind in his own work. So many new projects and avenues for Pendragon that he wanted to explore, but circumstances forced him to set them aside for the time being.

At midafternoon, the intercom on Blaine's desk buzzed, grabbing his attention. "Yes, Emily. What is it?"

"Your solicitor is calling, Mr. Reeves."

"Thanks, I've got it." He punched the flashing button on the phone. "Hello, Harry. What's up?"

"Our problems are over. Sir Geoffrey has withdrawn his interest in Sinclair. He was outranked. It looks like it's all yours."

"What do you mean *outranked*?"

"Everyone knows a Lord beats a Sir any day. And when it's not an empty title, when the Lord has lots of coin of the realm to go along with the title…"

Blaine's exasperation came out in his voice. "Could you give me the American translation? I don't seem to be grasping the British. What are you talking about?"

"It happened like this. Lord Easterfield told Sir Geoffrey, in the form of a hand delivered communiqué from my office, to immediately abandon any and all interest in the Sinclair deal or he'd spend whatever money necessary to ruin Sir Geoffrey financially. He even threatened to expose a few skeletons in Sir Geoffrey's closet as an added incentive."

"Who is Lord Easterfield, and why is he making threats on my behalf? What does he want from me?"

"Who is Lord Easterfield? Surely, you're jesting."

Blaine's voice changed from exasperation to irritation. "Do I sound like I'm *jesting*?"

"You mean you really don't know?"

The shock jolted Blain's reality as he listened to Harry's explanation. His mouth fell wide open in disbelief, then his response came as a barely audible whisper. "I had no idea."

Blaine sat in stunned silence for a few minutes after finishing his phone conversation with his attorney as he tried to collect his thoughts and make sense of the information. He grabbed the phone, dialed, and snapped out an order. "Get into my office right now."

A minute later, Dennis stood in the doorway, a puzzled expression on his face. "You growled, boss? I thought we had the Meg and Crista situation covered. Now what?"

"Suppose you tell me—" He tapped his pencil against his desktop as he looked Dennis squarely in the eyes. "—your Lordship."

Dennis closed the office door, then self-consciously glanced around the room before sitting in the chair opposite Blaine's desk. "So, Harry couldn't keep his mouth shut." A shy smile curled the edges of his lips as he gave an embarrassed shrug. "It's part of the inheritance from my Uncle Wilfred. Actually, there was a lot more to it than *just some money*."

"Apparently so. Why didn't you ever mention it?"

"I wasn't born with the title, and I wasn't raised with it. In fact, it had never occurred to me that I was in line for it. I just happened to be the closest male relative he had at the time he died. I guess I still feel a little self-conscious about the whole thing. I've always earned my own way. Besides, I practically had to beg you to hire me as it was. If you'd known about the title you never would have given me the time of day, let alone the job."

"Hire you! You could have bought me a million times over and even with your extravagant and expensive lifestyle, apparently you still can." Blaine shook his head in disbelief. "I don't know what to say. I don't understand."

"There's nothing to say."

"But why did you do it? Sir Geoffrey could have been really big trouble for you. No one goes out of their way looking for that kind of trouble."

A hard look crossed Dennis' face. "Well, let's just say I owed Sir Geoffrey one from years past. This seemed like a good and proper way to pay him back." His expression brightened. "Now, I don't suppose you'd like to tell me what all of this hush-hush stuff is really about, what's going on here."

A broad smile covered Blaine's face. "So, apparently Harry can keep his mouth shut after all. As employer to employee, it's still none of your business at this time. I don't suppose you'd want to tell me about you and Sir Geoffrey."

Dennis studied Blaine for a moment as if turning the matter over in his mind, then finally answered him. "As you know, I used to work for Sir Geoffrey's publishing firm. One day he made a move on me."

Confusion clouded Blaine's mind. He looked at Dennis questioningly. "What are you talking about? Is that some sort of British expression I'm not familiar with?"

"Very few people know that Sir Geoffrey is gay."

"But why would he make a move on you? Did he think you—"

"That's immaterial to him. He likes to exercise control and power over people. Now, I had no problem with him being gay. I'm a live and let live type of chap."

Dennis' face turned hard and distorted with anger. "But the day he walked up to me, shoved me against his office wall, and grabbed my crotch…well, reflex action took over. I punched him in the stomach so hard that it knocked him across the room. After he got his breath back and stopped retching, he just sat there on the floor laughing at me. He told me he'd give me two days to reconsider his *proposition*. If I didn't come around to his point of view, he'd see to it that I never worked in the publishing business again."

That one experience with Sir Geoffrey had solidly reinforced his approach with women. It was mutually agreeable, what both of them wanted or it didn't happen. Yet another hard jab of guilt assaulted his senses, disgust with himself about his totally unacceptable behavior with Meg. Unlike most women who were sexually harassed at work, he was in a position to protect himself and put an instant stop to the situation even though Sir Geoffrey was rich, powerful, and his employer.

"That was at eleven o'clock in the morning. I was in your office by one o'clock that afternoon. I thought that being American you wouldn't be intimidated by his title or any threat he would make. The inner workings of the British class system and aristocracy wouldn't be important to you or have any meaning. What Sir Geoffrey didn't know was that my Uncle Wilfred had unexpectedly died, leaving me in an extremely secure financial position."

Blaine started to say something, but Dennis held up his hand to stop him. "I am, as you Americans say, *on a roll,* so let me finish. I don't think Sir Geoffrey has ever gotten over the fact that his attempt to control me backfired. In fact, I suspect whatever it is he's trying to do to you is partly an attempt to get back at me. He's petty and extremely vindictive."

Dennis tried to suppress the mischievous grin tugging at the corners of his mouth. "Now, I really couldn't let him get away with that, could I?"

Blaine sat in silence, staring at Dennis. A look of new understanding passed between the two men, the growth of a new dimension to their relationship.

"There's no question that I've enjoyed the money," Dennis continued, "but I never really took this lordship thing that seriously the way other people do. There are those who have fancy and old established titles, including the large land estate that had been in the family for generations, even centuries in some cases, but there isn't any wealth to support it. Fortunately for me, that wasn't Uncle Wilfred's situation. He had the extreme wealth without the expensive burden of the country estate or castle."

Blaine slowly shook his head in disbelief. "I never would have guessed."

Dennis stood up and leaned forward with the palms of his hands spread against the top of Blaine's desk. He leveled a very serious look at Blaine. "One more thing. I wandered into your office that afternoon because, as I said, you were American and I assumed impervious to Sir Geoffrey's title and threats. I certainly didn't *need* a job. When I told you I wanted to work for you because I liked what you wanted to do and how you wanted to accomplish it, that was the absolute truth."

The two men again looked at each other for a long moment. Finally Dennis spoke in an upbeat tone. "I was busy when you so rudely demanded my presence in your office. I've a lot of work to do. See you later." He gave Blaine a wink and a breezy wave of his hand as he walked out the door.

Blaine worked very late that night trying to get all caught up and a little ahead so he would have some time when Meg got back. He finally arrived home at nine-thirty. His apartment was dark…and empty. He collapsed in bed and immediately fell into a sound sleep.

The next morning, Blaine sat in his living room sipping his coffee and reading the paper when Crista came in carrying her overnight bag.

"I thought you were only going out for dinner. Well, did you and Dennis have room service in one of the city's finest hotels?"

She set her bag on the floor and gave him a strange look. "Do you know where Dennis lives?"

Caution immediately took hold of his senses. "Yes…why do you ask?"

"Because I was shocked when he took me to his house last night. He lives in Belgravia. Isn't that one of the most expensive areas in London? Just how much money did he inherit?"

Blaine's genuine surprise showed on his face. "Dennis took you to his house? To the best of my knowledge he's never taken any of his dates to his house. I'm one of very few people who knows where Dennis lives. None of his dates, casual social acquaintances, or even the majority of his business associates know. He always claimed if any of his dates ever found out he could afford to live in Belgravia, he wouldn't be able to get rid of them. He always goes to their place or checks into a hotel."

Blaine gave her a very serious look. "I'm not sure exactly what this means, but it would appear Dennis is much more serious about you than I realized, more serious than I've ever seen him about any woman."

"Really? Do you really think so?" An inward smile slowly reached out and curled the edges of her lips as she picked up her bag and carried it to her room.

Blaine hurried to his office the next morning. He had two very important business meetings to conduct and a desk full of work. He didn't return home until late that night.

He woke early Thursday morning. Crista came out of her room just in time to see Blaine grab his raincoat and an umbrella. "Where are you off to in such a hurry? It's only six-thirty in the morning." She glanced out the window. "And it's raining."

"Meg comes back today. I want to make sure I can get my desk cleared off at a decent hour, so I can take her out to dinner. I have tons of paperwork to do and meetings with lawyers and accountants. We're wrapping up this business deal I've been working on for the past three months. As soon as everything is settled, I'll tell you all about it. I'm really excited about this project." He shot her an impish grin. "It might even have some benefits for you, too."

****

Meg arrived at her London hotel suite about three-thirty Thursday afternoon. As soon as she opened the door to her suite, she saw the message light blinking on the phone. She checked the message. It was from Crista. She immediately returned the call.

"Crista, it's Meg. I just got back and picked up your message. What can I do for you?"

Crista's voice conveyed a hint of urgency. "I'd like to come over right now. I need to talk to you. That is, if you're not too tired."

"Of course. Come right over."

"Thanks, Meg. I'll see you in a few minutes."

By the time she finished unpacking and putting everything away, Meg heard a knock at her door. She ushered Crista into the suite. "What's all this about?"

"I wanted to talk to you before you saw Blaine tonight."

A jolt of grave concern struck her. Anxiety churned in her stomach, and she felt her eyes widen in fright. She couldn't keep her growing panic out of her voice. "Blaine is okay, isn't he? Nothing has happened to him?"

"Blaine is fine—at least physically."

Meg looked at her questioningly. "What do you mean *at least physically*?"

"Pardon my impertinence, but I have to ask. Do you love him?"

Meg looked down at the floor, then out the rain streaked windows at the gloomy day. She finally turned back toward Crista. "I don't know what to do or think. I'm afraid. He hasn't offered me any kind of commitment for the future. I gave him my love, my heart, and my trust ten years ago and believed he loved me as much as I loved him even though he had never said so. He turned his back on that love, betrayed my trust, and broke my heart into a million pieces. I thought I was going to die. After I arrived in London, I found out he had been sleeping with another woman at the same time we were together in what I foolishly believed was a committed relationship. That knowledge brutally ripped open all the old wounds."

She blinked away the tears forming in her eyes. "I'm afraid, Crista. I don't think I'm strong enough to live through Blaine doing that to me again."

Crista looked squarely at Meg. "I think Blaine would give his life for you. That's how much he loves you. You two really aren't communicating at all. Have you ever been to his home?"

"No. He wanted to take me there, but I turned him down."

"He's not there right now. Come with me. I want to show you something."

Crista took Meg on a tour of Blaine's flat, showing her his collection of everything covering her career then the two photographs Blaine had purchased.

Meg took it all in, her attention moving from one item to another as a sense of awe filled her reality. "I remember when those photographs sold. Both were purchased by anonymous buyers for more money than they should have brought. Blaine bought both of them?"

Meg returned her attention to the oil painting that she had spotted as soon as she entered the living room. "I still can't believe this. I really can't believe this."

"Blaine painted that right after you arrived in London."

She continued to stare at the painting, lost in the feelings and emotions it conveyed.

"Do you like it?" The sound of a smooth masculine voice broke the silence of the room.

Meg whirled around and saw Blaine framed in the

front door. The intense emotion of the moment surged through her body. She smiled. "Yes, I do. I like it very much."

They looked at each other from across the room. The breath caught in her lungs. Her heart beat a little faster. She wasn't sure what to say or do. "I, uh…I didn't know you still painted."

"This is the first thing I've done in several years."

The room seemed to darken. All detail faded into a blurred background except for the golden glow radiating between Meg and Blaine. They locked into each other with an intensity that caused the very air to crackle. He walked toward her, his movements reminiscent of a dreamlike trance from a movie scene.

She stood riveted to the spot, unable to take her eyes off him. Unable to catch her breath. As he moved closer to her, wild surges of yearning coursed through her veins. Her very soul burned with her desire for Blaine, surpassed only by her overpowering love for him. A love she couldn't deny even if she wanted to. A love that had never died.

Blaine reached her side. As he tangled his fingers through her hair, he spoke in a soft voice. "I'm glad you like the painting." He lowered his head and brushed his lips tenderly against hers. "It was a labor of love."

Taking her trembling body gently in his arms, he captured her mouth with an emotional kiss. She put her arms around his neck while returning his kiss, pressing her body tightly against his.

Crista walked to the front door, then turned toward Blaine and Meg. "I'll hang out the Do Not Disturb sign on my way out." She left, closing the front door behind her.

Blaine smiled as he brushed his fingers across her cheek. "I thought she'd never leave."

He scooped Meg up in his arms, quickly covering the distance to his bedroom. He placed her gently on his bed. "I've never made love with anyone in this room, on this bed. I've been saving it for the woman I love very much. I've been saving it for you."

She put her arms around his neck and spoke in a very quiet voice, touched with just a hint of hesitancy. "Blaine...I love you." Once the words were out of her mouth the rest of her emotions poured out nonstop. "I've always loved you. I loved you from the first time I saw you. When you walked out of my life, I tried to delete you from reality. I wanted nothing more than to forget you ever existed, to erase you from my conscious memory. But I couldn't—"

She tried to swallow her anxiety. "I tried, but I couldn't stop loving you."

The moisture glistened in his eyes. He wrapped his arms around her and drew her tightly against his body, smothering her face and neck with kisses. "Marry me, Megan. Marry me now. I want you to be my wife. I want us to be together always, legally united for the rest of our lives."

Tears of happiness streamed down her cheeks. An almost uncontrollable joy welled in her heart. "Yes, Blaine, yes."

They remained lost in each other's arms as the rain stopped and the room took on a soft glow from the emerging light. His words tickled across her ear. "Let's get married immediately."

She looked lovingly into his eyes as she drew her finger across his cheek and over his upper lip. "Why are you in such a hurry?"

"I want this all legal and finalized before you can change your mind."

"I won't change my mind. But we have lots to talk about, decisions to make. We live half a world apart."

"Megan, we'll do whatever you want, but can we please discuss it in the morning?" He captured her mouth again. She eagerly responded to his kiss as the last fleeting moments of daylight disappeared and darkness permeated the bedroom.

****

The clock read five-thirty in the morning when Blaine kissed Meg on the cheek and gently shook her shoulder. "Meg, wake up. I have to be in my office by seven o'clock. I have an early meeting with my attorney. Do you want to stay here, or should I drop you back at your hotel on my way to work?"

"I'd better get up, too. You can drop me off at my hotel." She slipped out of bed and looked around. "I could use some coffee. Do you have a robe or something I can put on?"

He handed her one of his large T-shirts. She pulled it on, the hem falling halfway down her thighs toward her knees. Meg padded barefoot across the living room and into the kitchen to find the coffee pot.

"I thought I heard someone up and about."

Meg turned at the sound of Crista's voice.

"Here, let me help you. I know where everything is." Crista started to make the coffee then turned back to Meg. "Well?"

Meg couldn't contain her joy any longer. She threw her arms around Crista and gave her a big hug. "He asked me to marry him. In fact, he wants to get married

211

immediately, as soon as possible."

Crista returned her hug. "I'm so happy for you. There's never been two people who belong together more than you and Blaine."

"Well, no one's going to get any coffee this way." Blaine broke into their conversation.

Crista walked over to her brother and gave him a big hug. "I'm so happy for you and Meg. This has been a long time coming. In fact, it's long overdue."

Blaine grinned. "If one of you women will actually make coffee, I'll take a shower and get ready for work."

Crista threw a kitchen towel at Blaine who ducked and quickly left the room as she yelled after him. "Blaine Reeves, don't you dare turn into a chauvinist."

He quickly crossed the living room with his hands up in the air in a gesture of surrender. Meg's and Crista's laughter trailed him across the room.

Following breakfast, Blaine dropped Meg off at her hotel and continued to his office. He had a three-hour meeting with Harry and Sinclair's lawyers. He emerged from the meeting all smiles as the lawyers left. He walked down the hall to Meg's temporary office where she busily worked on the material from the countryside shoot.

She looked up as he entered the office. "You look very pleased with yourself. I assume your meeting went well."

He kissed her on the cheek. "It couldn't have gone better. I'll have a great announcement to make later concerning the company's expansion." He put his arms around her and continued to hold her. "Now, I want to talk about our wedding. What do you want, a large wedding in the States or a small intimate service here in

London? Needless to say, a large wedding in the States will take several months to plan. A small, intimate wedding here in London could be right away. It's up to you."

"I've been thinking about it all morning. I have no family to speak of, and my friends are scattered all over the country. You've lived in London for the last ten years, so I assume you don't have close friends in the States. Unless you've made up with your father, the only close family you have is Crista, and she's here right now. So…why don't we just have that small intimate wedding sometime next week?"

He broke out in a very big grin and pulled her body tightly against his. "That's perfect. I couldn't be happier."

He started to kiss her just as Dennis walked in. "Don't you two think you're setting a bad example for the rest of us lowly employees? What if everyone behaved like that in the office? No one would get any work done."

He held out his hand to Blaine. "I hear congratulations are in order." The two men shook hands.

Dennis turned to Meg. "Allow me to be the first to kiss the bride." He gave her a warm but innocent friendly kiss on the lips. "Best wishes, Meg. I know you two will be very happy."

Dennis turned his attention to both of them. "Crista suggests, and she's right as usual, that we should take you two to dinner tonight to celebrate. How about it?"

Blaine looked questioningly at Meg who nodded. "We'd love it. That will be a good time for me to make another little announcement." He grinned impishly, directing his comment specifically to Dennis. "Make sure you take us someplace very expensive."

Dennis turned his attention to Meg. "Enough of this for right now. We have business to handle. Come on, luv. Let's see what you have for me from the first countryside section."

Blaine kissed her on the cheek. "I'll see you later."

She motioned toward the computer as she turned her attention to the work at hand. "Here are the pictures I've identified so far and here is the rough draft copy that I've put together. I'll finish the rest of the picture identification while you look over what I've written. I took into consideration the type of changes you suggested from the London chapter when I wrote this." They both sat down and went to work, going right through lunch and continuing for the rest of the afternoon.

That evening Meg, Blaine, Crista, and Dennis occupied an intimate table in a quiet corner of an elegant restaurant enjoying a bottle of champagne. Dennis and Crista had toasted Meg and Blaine's upcoming wedding.

Meg turned to Blaine. "You said something this morning about another announcement, something to do with the company. Would you like to enlighten us?"

"This is probably as good a time as any. Today, I signed the final papers consummating the deal for Pendragon to purchase Sinclair Publishing, a small literary imprint in New York.

Meg and Crista beamed their surprise and pleasure. Dennis, on the other hand, displayed shock. "You bought an American publishing company? That's what all the secret meetings have been about?"

Blaine grinned and turned his attention to Dennis. "I thought I might send you to New York as soon as the travel book is completed. You would be there for at least a month, maybe longer, to head up the transition and whip the company into shape. Are you interested?"

Dennis gave Crista a quick wink. "I think I'll be able to work that into my busy schedule."

Blaine leaned over to Meg and kissed her tenderly on the lips. "Is this the part where it says we live happily ever after?"

Meg looked lovingly into Blaine's eyes as she slowly drew her finger across his upper lip. "Yes, that's exactly what we'll be doing."

A word about the author…

I've lived most of my life in Los Angeles and earned my living for twenty years by working in television production. I was always interested in writing and dabbled at it, but not seriously. I combined my interest in writing with my avocation of photography and began doing magazine articles featuring my photographs. After selling several articles, I discovered I enjoyed the writing process as much as the photography.

My friends told me I should make use of my television contacts and write scripts. I enrolled in a screen writing class at UCLA. By the close of class I knew screen writing was not for me. The other thing I knew was that I wanted to write novels rather than magazine articles.

www.samanthagentry.com
www.shawnadelacorte.com

Thank you for purchasing
this publication of The Wild Rose Press, Inc.

For questions or more information
contact us at
info@thewildrosepress.com.

The Wild Rose Press, Inc.
www.thewildrosepress.com